The Ghost of Glenmellish

Some other books by Pat Gerber

FICTION
Stranger on the River

NON-FICTION
The Stone of Destiny
Outdoors Scotland

The Ghost of Glenmellish

A NOVEL OF SPINE-TINGLING SPOOKINESS
SET IN A SCOTTISH GLEN

PAT GERBER

For Jamie, with love

Text © Pat Gerber 2001
Illustrations © Sue Gerber 2001

First published in 2001 by Kailyards Press, Glasgow.

This edition published in 2002 by:
Glowworm Books Ltd, Unit 7, Greendykes Industrial Estate,
Broxburn, West Lothian, EH52 6PG, Scotland.

Telephone: 01506-857570
Fax: 01506-858100
URL: http://www.glowwormbooks.co.uk

ISBN 1 871512 82 4

Printed and bound in Poland

Reprint Code   10   9   8   7   6   5   4   3   2   1

Contents

Acknowledgements

Several people and organisations have given of their time and knowledge to help me with this book. In particular, I would like to thank Bryony Carnie for being an invaluable plot consultant, critic and dog expert. Thanks also to Auchindrain Museum, Inveraray, the children of Primary 6, Braidbar Primary School, Giffnock and their teachers Susan Brass and Carole Buchanan, to Mary Baxter, Margot Delaney, Narinder Dhami, Cyril Gerber, Janice Lindsay, Martin MacIntyre, Jennifer Macleod, Robyn Marsack and Liffy Grant.

GHOST

Annie first saw the ghost one evening in May.

After their evening meal Dad washed the dishes while Annie began her homework. He said, 'Will you lock up the cottages tonight?'

Annie pleaded, 'When I've done this?' She hadn't written anything so far.

'Okay, but you'll want to be home before dark.' He hung a mug on its hook. 'Tell Mum I'll be busy in the Visitor Centre till bedtime. Got to keep it tidy. You never know, a Tourist Board inspector might decide to drop by – I wish.' He went out.

Mum appeared, her arms full of sheep's wool. 'How's it going, love?' She peered over Annie's shoulder and read out the teacher's notes, 'Write a story called *The Journey*.'

Annie chewed the end of her pencil. 'I'm stuck.'

'A journey, hmm?' The kettle whistled on the cooker. Mum poured boiling water into a tub, almost vanishing behind clouds of steam. 'Well, you could write about the day we moved here. Remember?'

Annie gazed into the swirling steam. As if by magic, her pencil set off across the page slowly at first, then gathering speed. *A year ago we left the city for ever. Mum and Dad chucked their jobs and bought Auchentibart Museum here in Glenmellish. The jeep broke down at Loch Lomond. Dad phoned the AA but Mum and I hitched a lift in the removal van. It smelled of diesel. The driver stopped at a transport caff and bought me a fried egg roll. It burst all down my front.*

The story went on by itself over two and a half pages and ended, *We got here at midnight, it was pitch black. There were no street lights! I had to sleep on the floor. Next morning I couldn't believe my eyes. I thought a Museum was a dusty old building but here were all these wee cottages scattered about and fields in between with sheep and cows and hens and rusty old ploughs. I love living at Auchentibart Museum of Country Life. Even though it's sometimes scary in the darkness. Now I never want to live anywhere else. And I'll get a dog, maybe a Dalmatian, or a Collie.* She sat back and looked at her work. She'd put in lots of full stops. Mrs McCrindle, the teacher, really liked full stops.

When Annie looked up, Mum was stirring the tub whilst holding a paperback novel in the other hand, deeply engrossed in the story. Annie thought how Mum was changing. In the city, she used to dress neatly in black for work.

Annie put her homework away. She yawned. 'I'm to lock up tonight.'

'Okay, love.'

Annie got the torch out of the drawer and took down bunches of keys. The wellies felt cold on her bare feet. She opened the back door. Half of her couldn't be bothered doing this. The other half felt that it was quite grown-up, being trusted to lock the cottages to stop thieves and vandals getting in, that she was part of Mum and Dad's working life here. None of her friends got to do stuff like this, except perhaps Sadie Munro.

Outside, the setting sun made streaks of pink, gold and lilac in the clouds. The rain had stopped and the air smelled of herbs and sheep droppings. The wet track glistened like a silver ribbon, leading past the henhouse, over a little green hill, around the first five cottages, then across a wee bridge to the sixth one. Beyond, the land rose to endless moors.

'Baaahaa!' Hot-Pot the sheep bleated hopefully, trotting after her.

'Sorry, Hot-Pot, no bread. Shoooh!' Annie waved her arms at the sheep. It had been an orphaned lamb last year, brought into the kitchen and hand-reared till it turned mischievous. Now it was supposed to live on grass with the rest of the flock, but preferred people – and toast.

Annie reached the hen-pen. All six hens were safely inside their house, clucking softly. She closed the little hatch and padlocked the gate. Foxes were fond of chicken dinners, especially at night, so you had to make sure they couldn't get in.

She hurried along the path checking that the cottage doors were firmly padlocked. Some of the locks were stiff and could pinch your fingers. Daylight was failing now and vapour was rising from the ground. She sang softly to herself to keep from being scared, and switched on the torch. But the beam made the streaks of mist look like writhing ghosts.

The torchlight began to flicker. Oh no, the battery was giving out. Street lamps would be nice, she thought. The last orange glimmer wavered over the rough bark of a huge tree that grew beside the burn, a Scots Pine hundreds of years old. She tried not to remember that it was supposed to have been used as a gallows in times gone by. The only sounds were her own breathing and the trickling of the river. She couldn't help adding the imaginary creaking of a rope with a hanged felon dangling from it. What was a felon? Some sort of crim? Pocketing the useless torch, she gave herself a shake, conjuring up Mum's voice – "Come on, Annie, there's work to be done". She shuffled onto the bridge.

Her foot felt a small heap. What was it? She couldn't see properly. A jersey or something dropped by a visitor? She picked it up and stuffed it inside her jacket; the owner would be looking for it. Oh, yeuch, it smelled of cow dung.

A little rush of cold wind made her shiver.

The full moon appeared, casting silveryness over everything. Well, at least she could see a bit now. She started up the path.

On a little incline, half hidden by a yew tree, loomed the Auld Hoose, oldest cottage of the museum. The knobbly stone walls splayed out and the thatched roof was so scruffy it made the house look like a tousle-haired boy.

Annie felt in her pocket for the key.

Now the wind was rising, playing scary tricks with her. Surely these sucky sounds must be the squelching of some-one's feet in the marshy ground? And weren't these airy murmurs breathy voices like – like the whisperings of wraiths?

Moonlight weaving through the branches made creepy shadows flutter along the wall. Or were they wispy people drifting around in shades of grey like – like pieces of torn tissue-paper? And there – was it a boy with untidy hair? Could he be looking at her? She rubbed her eyes, trying to get him into focus but softly, before she could be certain of

anything, the shapes drifted away like dead leaves on the night air, till only the faintest whiff of peat-smoke remained.

Clink! She'd dropped the keys. Freaking out completely, she leaped back over the bridge. Tripping, crashing into objects, she hurtled homewards.

TROUBLE

Annie slammed the back door shut behind her. She leaned against it, breathless, kicking off her wellies, fighting the images that crowded her mind.

'Everything okay?' Mum's voice was reassuringly normal. The smells of hot wool and cooking greens wafted around the kitchen.

Annie gasped, 'It's horrible out there.'

'What's up?' Mum put her book down.

Trying to get a grip on herself, Annie said, 'It was *so* spooky. The torch battery gave out. I thought there were people – '

'Oh Annie, cool down. You and your imagination! And put a new battery in before you forget.'

Annie's breathing quietened as she rummaged for batteries. Everything was always nice and normal and cosy around Mum. The misty shreds of people slowly faded from her mind.

'What's that Annie, sticking out of your jacket?'

Annie pulled out a ragged woollen shirt. 'I found it on the wee bridge. It's manky.'

Mum glanced at it, wrinkling her nose. 'Amazing, the stuff visitors drop. They'll phone weeks later, and expect me to post it to them.'

Annie peered into the tub Mum was stirring. Wool swirled about like greeny-yellow hair. 'What's this for?'

'Tomorrow's textile workshop.'

Annie helped heave the tub up on to the draining board. 'Yuck. Spinach.' She grimaced at a heap of steaming leaves.

'Not spinach. Woad.' Mum tipped out the dye.

'Yeuchy colour,' said Annie.

Mum pulled on pink rubber gloves and began to lift out the wool. 'Watch what happens when the oxygen in the air hits it.' Sure enough, the wool gradually began to turn turquoise blue. 'Jo-Ellen wanted to see this. Isn't it magic?'

Dad came through from the Visitor Centre, carrying a parcel. 'Where *is* our resident Canadian?'

Mum said, 'Jo-Ellen? Still working. She found some fascinating facts in the archive at Ardmellish House and didn't want to stop.'

'What's an archive?' Annie hadn't quite made up her mind whether or not she liked their ancient crumbly lodger, Jo-Ellen.

'An archive is a store of old documents and things, bits of evidence from the past. And though the Hassan family are new to Ardmellish House, they've inherited its library and an archive that must go back hundreds of years.' Dad tore open the parcel. 'Take a look at these. Your idea, Annie. What do you think?' He pulled out a handful of brightly coloured publicity leaflets and spread them on the table. He smiled. 'We'll keep some of these for *our* archive, so people in the future will – '

Annie pounced on them. 'Great! The green lettering's just right.' She read out, *'AUCHENTIBART MUSEUM OF COUNTRY LIFE. Find out how your farming ancestors lived and worked. Auchentibart is a fermtoun or communal village of great antiquity, one of the few in Scotland to have survived, much as it always was, on its original site in a lovely Highland glen.* Can I take some to school tomorrow?'

'Good idea,' said Dad. 'Get your mates to put them in the places their parents work?'

Annie stuffed a bundle into her schoolbag along with her homework. 'Oh yeah? Like the Wildlife Centre? Don't think so.'

Dad smiled bitterly. 'The Wildlife Centre catches all the tourists from Ardmellish village before they reach us.'

Mum thought for a minute. 'The library will take some I'm sure. And the Tourist Office.'

Dad said quietly, 'The Wildlife Centre got two Visitor Attraction stars in last year's guidebook. We haven't even got a mention.' He looked down. 'That's why we're beginning to think about giving up.'

Annie's heart missed a beat. She'd had enough frights for one night. 'Giving up?'

Mum began wringing out clods of wool. She glared at Dad. 'Keith, we weren't going to mention this till things were more definite.'

Annie said, 'More definite? Dad, what's been going on?'

'You won't like this, Annie, but – we've written to ask about teaching jobs back in the city.'

This was too much for Annie. 'But you said we were going to give it three years.'

'Calm down, Annie,' said Mum. 'Nothing's been decided yet. We wouldn't do anything without telling you.'

'You just have,' Annie glared at her parents. 'But you said

we'd always discuss things as a *family* now.'

Dad's voice was almost a whisper. 'I – we didn't want to upset you.'

Annie fired up, 'You two keeping *secrets* upsets me.'

Dad went on, 'Remember Opening Day at Easter? Even with the local press covering us, only three people turned up.'

'But it was pouring with rain, Easter weekend,' protested Annie. 'And now we've got these three bus tour bookings in.'

Dad put his head in his hands.

Mum said, 'It does seem a shame. The Museum's so nearly a going concern.'

'That's just the trouble. The only way we're going is downhill.' Dad sighed.

Annie jumped up, knocking the leaflets onto the floor. 'I can't believe you're giving in.'

Dad argued, 'We're not making enough money, even with Jo-Ellen's room-rental. Last year was a disaster and if the weather doesn't pick up, this one won't be any better – '

Mum said, 'Without a mention in the tourist guidebook, no one can find out about us.'

Annie opened her mouth to protest again, but the phone rang.

'Keith, can you take it?' Mum dumped the dripping wool in the sink.

Dad talked for a minute on the phone then said, 'Thanks for letting us know.'

Mum said, 'Letting us know what?'

He put the phone down. 'Well. How ironic. Apparently an inspector may be among your students tomorrow.'

'What sort of inspector?' Annie shoved the crumpled shirt away and started picking up the scattered leaflets.

Dad took a bottle of beer from the fridge and sat down at the table. 'A Tourist Board inspector. Incognito. At last.'

'Incog-what?'

'Nito,' said Mum. 'We're not supposed to know they're coming to assess us, so's the inspector isn't given special treatment. That way they find out how we really treat the public, see?'

Annie watched Mum, who wasn't sounding all that keen on giving up. Maybe this inspection would give her a glimmer of hope. She helped herself to a slice of bread and a banana.

Mum started rinsing the wool under the running tap, splashing cold water everywhere. 'It's vital we get as high a rating as we can. If we get into next year's listings, more people will be able to find us.'

Dad went on, 'The Museum would literally be on the map.'

Mum said, 'Easier to sell, you mean?' She squeezed and pummelled the wool as if it had annoyed her. 'And we need to make it clear that visitors to this Museum have to be the sort who enjoy wandering about in all weathers.'

Dad gazed moodily into his beer. 'So we have to get our advertising to the sort of people who don't mind a wee drop of rain. Annie, is everything locked up?'

Suddenly remembering why she'd run through the darkness to the safety of home, Annie began to feel shaky again. 'Y-yes. Well, that is, I did lock everything except – the Auld Hoose.' She ended lamely, 'I dropped the keys. And I couldn't see – '

Mum tutted, 'Och Annie, we must be able to rely on you to do things properly.'

'Sorry.'

'Well, I suppose Dad'll finish up for once. Time for bed, you've got school in the morning.'

'Oh no, Monday. Murdo Clerk, big bully, might be on the bus.' Annie made a face meant to look like Murdo. In fact she really was scared of the farmer's big red-faced son. 'I hope he's been dropped in sheep-dip and has to be off school for years.'

'Annie!' said Dad. 'Bed.'

The front door latch clicked open. 'Yoohoo,' called a voice, 'it's only me.' Jo-Ellen hobbled in.

She was a small woman with a big head, like a garden gnome. Annie didn't quite like her foosty smell, sort of tobacco mixed with old shoes. She had brown wrinkly skin like crushed tissue paper. And her bright, bold eyes seemed to see right through you.

When Annie went to say her goodnights, Dad, Mum and Jo-Ellen were comfortably ensconced round the kitchen table drinking tea. Dad was reading the paper, Mum was handing the grotty shirt to Jo-Ellen. 'Look at this, for a nice piece of hand-weaving and stitching. Pretty old – what do you think?'

Jo-Ellen reached out claw-like fingers. 'Indeed. Was it made here, eh?'

'Annie found it when she was locking up.'

Jo-Ellen's hand stopped in mid-air. 'Found it?'

The shirt fell from Mum's hand.

'Yes,' said Annie, 'on the wee bridge.'

The shirt lay spreadeagled on the floor, its torn arms flung up as if in fright.

Jo-Ellen hissed, 'You gotta burn that.' Then as though to herself, 'Fire is the only answer.' Her beady eyes bored into Annie's.

Frightened by the old woman's intensity Annie stammered, 'Why? We can't just burn someone's shirt. They must have left it by mistake. They might come back.'

'Left it, eh? Come back? Oh they are so clever. Honey, you

21

must *never* pick up unexplained bundles of clothing!' Jo Ellen shoved the shirt away with her foot as if it was too dangerous to touch. 'Didn't you know, this is how dead people try to make contact with the living?'

'Dead people?' Annie shivered, remembering the shadowy figures fluttering along the Auld Hoose wall.

'Yes, dead people try to get you to pick up their clothes. And if you do, they'll haunt you – '

Mum said mildly, 'Oh Jo-Ellen, stop teasing Annie. She won't sleep a wink. More tea anyone?'

But Jo-Ellen wasn't laughing.

This was the worst scare of all. Annie grabbed the shirt from the floor and fled to her room.

BULLY

Annie lay awake for ages trying to remember exactly what she'd seen. Shadows shifted through her memory but she couldn't catch hold of an image. Had she imagined that boy with the messy hair?

He drifted through her dreams all night, appearing and disappearing round the corner of her eye, till she was woken by the sound of the cock crowing.

In the bathroom she splashed cold water over her face. The radio was blaring out the seven o'clock news in the kitchen, while Mum made toast.

Annie took down the mug with the sheepdog's face on and filled it with milk. 'Mum, can we get a dog soon? You promised if we came here?'

'Well, if we decided to stay in the country. But now – '

Annie knew all the arguments inside out. She yawned. 'Er – Mum?'

'Mmm?' Mum dropped a piece of toast onto Annie's plate. It smelled lovely.

'Do people really leave their ghosts behind when they die?'

Mum shook her head, laughing. 'Oh Annie, whatever next?' She buttered her own slice of toast then said more thoughtfully, 'No one *knows* exactly what happens when someone dies, so people *believe* different things. Maybe, if it's someone you love, you feel better believing their spirit somehow goes on existing. Maybe it really happens. But me, I think one just dies like a daffodil does, end of story.'

'But – Jo-Ellen said – '

'Jo-Ellen?' Mum's voice dropped to a whisper. 'Love, Jo-Ellen's what they call "fey", into folk-lore and ghostie stories and rubbish like that. Don't let her get to you.'

'You won't let her burn my shirt?'

'*Your* shirt is it now?' Mum smiled. 'Certainly not. Too

good an example of hand-weaving,' Mum waved her toast at the washing machine. 'But grubby. I put it in with your stuff, while you were in the bathroom. It'll be fresh for the real owner, if he comes back. If not, we might display it in the Visitor Centre.'

For some reason Annie felt weird about this. She picked up her schoolbag. 'Do I have to open up?' She normally unlocked the cottages on her way out to the bus stop, but today she didn't want to.

'Please, love.' Mum took the wool down from the pulley. It looked light and fluffy and sky-blue now it was dry. 'But open *all* the cottages. Dad wasn't best pleased, having to finish off for you last night. If a job's worth – '

Dad wandered in with a sheaf of leaflets. '*Is* a job worth doing, that's what I'm wondering, these days. You off, Annie?'

She grabbed her jacket. 'Yup. See you, Dad.'

'I've scheduled you for the Auld Hoose after school. There's a busload due in around four o'clock and – things need watching.'

'The Auld Hoose?' Annie's voice faltered. Unlocking was one thing, spending a couple of hours alone there might be scary.

'Yes. I'm on at the Visitor Centre and Mum's busy.'

Outside, tiny droplets of water glistened on the new grass. Annie broke a fingernail opening the henhouse and stood biting the ragged edge while five black hens and the bright brown cock marched out, squawking softly.

Hairy Highland cows munched grass in the field, four orange and one black, with wide and dangerous-looking horns. A little flock of sheep wandered about, followed by their bleating lambs. Except for Hot-Pot, who stood gazing intently at her.

Annie fed her a toast crust. Hot-Pot baaed, following her hopefully till Annie shooed her away.

The Auld Hoose sat primly in the drizzle, as if it knew nothing about last night, or was keeping it a secret. She liked its two tiny windows with red chequered curtains made by Mum, and the plain wooden door in its squint frame and she used to daydream about the people who once lived and played here.

She undid the lock and pulled the creaky wooden door which, for some reason, opened outwards. She propped it in place with a heavy flat-iron. Inside there was only cool silence, and the familiar smells of mildew, mice and moss. Not a whiff of peat-smoke – well, the fire hadn't been lit since Gala Day last summer, so how could there be?

Oh! A scrabbly sound. She turned. Too late. Hot-Pot's hard head thudded into the back of her knees. 'Ouch!' She fell.

For a second she lay, slightly stunned, seeing stars, staring up at the huge stone lintel above the doorway, while Hot-Pot looked down at her with expressionless eyes, baaing loudly.

Annie shoved the sheep away. 'Go away, Hot-Pot. That's a really bad habit of yours.' She got up. 'How's about coming on the bus? Sort big Murdo out for us?' She tried to laugh, but the fright made her voice wobbly.

Today the bus was full, the windows all steamed up. Big Murdo and his pals were fooling about as usual, chucking their bags around. Annie hated the journey, with them all showing off and shouting and picking on the younger ones. She particularly hated big Murdo Clerk, with his red bony face and his pale eyes that stared at you, expressionless as cold grey stones.

The bus stopped at Duncan's road end. His wee black dog

stood at the roadside, looking on mournfully as he limped up the steps, her thin tail hung low. 'Away and catch a rabbit, Megabyte,' he called as the bus door shut. *'Tillidh mi an ceartuair*, I'll be back.'

Big Murdo shouted, 'Ho, here's Dafty Duncan.'

His cronies snorted derisively.

Murdo bawled, 'C'mon folks, gie the eejit a seat – if ye's don't mind the smell.'

'Shut it, Murdo,' Duncan spoke softly through his teeth as the bus lurched forward.

A schoolbag came whirling through the air and hit Duncan on the side of the head, knocking him to the ground. Suddenly Murdo was standing over him, cooing, 'Oh my, the poor wee laddie. He's fallen down. Whit a shame, eh folks? Whit a niff, eh folks?'

A nervous titter went round the bus. Everybody was afraid of big Murdo.

Annie glared up at the bully. 'Get lost Murdo.' She wanted to say he smelled of sheep dung himself, but didn't dare.

Murdo clamped a hand on Duncan's shoulder. 'Aw son, whit's up wi' ye? Did yer ma feed ye on lumpy porridge, eh?' He twisted Duncan's arm cruelly. 'She gied ye lumpy legs awright,' he sneered, swaggering to the back of the bus, laughing.

It was Sadie's stop next. She got on, followed by her big brother Coll. Annie breathed a sigh of relief. Coll would keep Murdo quiet.

Annie's heart burned with hurt for Duncan. He'd once told her how his mum and dad had died in the car crash that had left him crippled. Now he lived with his gran, who wore dungarees, lived on pickled beetroot and was a Gaelic singer.

Annie dragged Duncan onto the seat beside her. Glancing

at his tight mouth, she thought he was probably finding it difficult not to cry, so she gazed out of the window and talked, to give him some time to regain his cool. 'Guess what, I saw ghosts last night.' Then, exaggerating wildly, trying to make him laugh at her, she told him about finding the old shirt and the shreds of mist that had looked like people, especially a boy. She mimicked Jo-Ellen's horror, 'You must *nevrr* pick up bundles of clothing. It's the owner coming to *hahnt* you.' She began to feel better herself, till she ran out of words and there was a silence.

Taking a breath she rattled on, 'They said we had to publicise the museum more. We got these leaflets done. Look.' She pulled out the brightly coloured bundle. 'Mum and I designed them.'

Duncan sniffed and wiped his nose on his sleeve. He was recovering a bit, but maybe wouldn't want to talk yet.

She thought for a minute, then said, 'See dogs? My Mum said, "You could have a dog of your own if we lived in the countryside." Here we are – do I have a dog? Now all of a sudden we can't stay.'

Duncan looked startled. 'Are you leaving?'

'That's what they're saying. But I *really* like it here. The town was horrible. The school toilets stank. Everything was vandalised. There was *nowhere* you could play outside the flat.' Annie's voice drifted into silence as she remembered the grey streets where so much nameless danger lurked that your parents never let you out.

Soon the bus was swishing past the Wildlife Park, over the bridge, under the archway, along the shore road by the post office, and pulling up with a hiss of brakes.

Everyone pushed to get off, but big Murdo was too quick for them, as usual. He liked to 'help' each of them out by shoving them. Annie thought she'd dodged him, but he put out a foot and tripped her. She tumbled onto the roadway, her schoolbag burst open, and her leaflets flew out scattering in the gusty wind.

Her eyes filling with tears, she watched the leaflets flutter away, one by one. Some landed on a passing line of cars. A forestry lorry laden with pine trunks drove over the rest, flattening them onto the wet tarmac with its huge wheels, till the roadway was a mosaic of colour.

Duncan, who had also been pushed, picked himself up. 'Some of the leaflets are all right,' he said, beginning to peel a few off the road.

The bus moved away, with Murdo and his cronies making stupid faces at them through the windows.

Sadie stuck her tongue out. 'I'll get you, Murdo Clerk.' She waggled her fingers at him as the bus disappeared round a bend in the road.

Annie couldn't help laughing at her through the tears.

Clutching the remaining leaflets, they went into the school. Annie felt glad that Duncan had cheered up by now. Some people called him Dafty Duncan because he had a wobbly walk, but she knew he was clever.

'Duncan,' said Mrs McCrindle the teacher, nearly every morning, 'Anything new from the Internet?' For Duncan could do anything with a computer. He was brilliant at arithmetic too, but most of all he was a fantastic singer and could play dozens of tunes on his fiddle. Annie liked his quiet ways and the fact that he didn't boast all the time.

Sure enough, this morning Mrs McCrindle asked, 'Any luck on the Worldwide Web, Duncan?'

Duncan looked up, 'I put a new question on our web page. Maybe there'll be some hits tonight.'

'Excellent,' Mrs McCrindle smiled, dishing out piles of books, leaflets, photocopied papers and telephone

directories for them to rummage through.

They were working on local history. Annie liked imagining life in Glenmellish a hundred, two hundred years ago, when you had to walk everywhere, and there were no welly boots, no TV, you had horses and carts instead of buses, and there was no electricity to light and warm your home.

Today, Annie and Sadie were helping to turn a roll of wallpaper into a big chart called Hunt the Ancestor.

'An ancestor,' sang Mrs McCrindle, 'is a forefather – someone from whom you're descended, like your grandad.'

Sadie piped up, 'Can ye hae a foremother, Miss?'

Mrs McCrindle gave Sadie a look down through her specs, 'I don't think it's called that, exactly.'

'Well, isn't ma great-granny a ancestor, Miss?'

'*An* ancestor, Sadie. Yes of course,' said Mrs McCrindle. 'And have you done your interview with her yet?'

'Aw Miss, it's no' fair.' Sadie could make her voice really moany. 'I've spoke tae ma grannies and ma granddad. Naebody else has tae do a great-granny.'

The children had made a huge tree for the Ancestor chart, by sticking loads of scrunched-up green tissue onto a sheet of sky blue paper. There was a brown crepe paper trunk with a branch for each of the main family names in Glenmellish. They were trying to find out whose family had been living in Glenmellish the longest. So far, the farthest back were Munro, MacIntyre and Clerk, names which had been in Glenmellish since the late 1700s. Apart from Annie's surname, Campion, the newest name was Hassan, the wealthy family who'd bought Ardmellish House a couple of years back.

'Now, everyone,' Mrs McCrindle handed out photocopied sheets, 'these are from our minister, Mr MacIntyre. Ministers have often proved good collectors of local information. Mr MacIntyre kindly made us extra copies of our oldest parish records while he was helping your lodger I believe, Annie.'

'Jo-Ellen?'

'Indeed.'

Annie's mind began to wander as Mrs McCrindle went on to explain how parish records were books in which churches kept details of local happenings like births, marriages and deaths.

By lunchtime the rain had stopped and the sun came out. Annie went wandering along the beach with Sadie. Coming as a new pupil to Ardmellish Primary last summer term, Annie had found it difficult to make friends. Everyone else knew each other, and she'd felt a bit of an outsider to begin with. Sadie Munro was a bit of a loner and always wore droopy old clothes, but she was okay and recently they'd begun to hang out together most of the time.

Sadie said, 'What've you got?'

Annie prised open her sandwich and sniffed. 'Egg. The hens keep on laying. We get egg in *everything*.'

Sadie tore her roll in two. Some of the filling squidged out onto her fingers. She held out half. 'Swop? Mine's is salmon. We aye gets salmon. Ma's usin' up last year's fish out the freezer.' Mr Munro was the Ardmellish Estate ghillie – fishing for trout and salmon was his job.

Annie's mind was still on the past. 'How old's your great-granny?'

'She says she's as auld as the hills. Ninety-somethin'. Why?'

Annie tried to work something out in her head, but failed. 'So she'd be – like, the same age as us in – um – '

'Hunners o' years ago.' Sadie accepted an egg sandwich, bit into it and got some stuck on her cheeks.

Annie had never met the old lady. 'Can she remember stuff?'

Sadie spoke through a full mouthful, 'She's aye tellin' us what *her* granny said tae her when she was wee.'

Annie's brain cells were dancing reels, trying to do the sum. 'So *her* granny'd have been our age in – '

They reached Duncan, sitting on the sea-wall dangling his twisted legs over the edge. He said, 'If Sadie's great-gran's

in her nineties, she'd have been our age around 1920. That would make *her* granny our age maybe around the 1870s.'

'So,' said Annie, 'old Mrs Munro sort of joins now with then.'

Sadie looked at Duncan and shook her head.

Duncan said, 'Sort of.'

Annie felt pleased. 'Well, she might remember much more that just stories. She might know about *people*. Could we go and see her?'

Sadie shrugged, 'She's aye sayin' naebody bothers wi' her now she's got put awa' up at the home.' She skipped away along the beach. 'So she's comin' to stay wi' us for her holidays.'

Part of Sadie's problem, thought Annie, was that she never sounded enthusiastic about anything. Her voice was as limp as the grey school skirt that drooped round her skinny legs.

Trailing back towards school with Duncan, Annie said, 'Where is the old folks' home?'

'Up the hill. My gran sings there sometimes.' He stopped. 'Listen, Annie, about ghosts, I'll do a bit of surfing tonight, see if there's anything on the Internet about picking up clothes?'

'Oh, right.' But Annie wasn't sure if she wanted to remember all that, let alone think about her scary experience.

JOCK

By the time Annie got home she was tired out and hungry. In the museum car park were two cars and a bus. Tourists were strung out along the paths between the cottages.

The Visitor Centre smelt of coffee. It had big windows and shelves with books and brightly coloured souvenirs for sale. Annie's favourites were little china replicas of the museum's cottages. A big freezer held ice creams and drinks.

Dad said 'Had a good day? You can take your homework down to the Auld Hoose with you.'

'Can I get a drink first?'

'Of course.' Dad tore off two tickets for a couple of ancient tourists. 'There you are, Sir. And here's our information leaflet. It's free.'

The couple wandered into the Display Area.

Dad said, 'See, Annie, you can't tell who might steal. We've lost such a lot to petty thieves.'

Annie chose a drink from the fridge. What Dad said was true. Almost every week something would go missing from one of the cottages – a spoon, a tablecloth, a cup.

Each cottage was set out differently, to give an idea how the people had lived at different periods. Last winter, Mum had made curtains, had begged and borrowed coverings for the little box-beds and rag rugs for the hearths, even a doll for the Auld Hoose cradle. Local people had donated tablecloths and oil lamps and all sorts of items to make the houses look more lived-in. But just last week the big black kettle had disappeared. They'd no idea who had stolen it.

By the time she'd cycled down to the Auld Hoose, the bus tourists had gone. It was so quiet she could hear the nearby cows pulling the grass and eating it. The sun was warm and a couple of hens clucked contentedly around, scratching for beetles and worms in the ground. High above her head a lark sang, whirring up and down above its hidden nest as if it was on elastic.

Annie got out her homework, but soon her mind was drifting to what it would have been like living here long ago. The summer smells would have been the same – well, except for diesel-smoke from passing lorries. The sounds from animals and birds would have been the same too. But the whole way you spent your life would have been so different.

The aged couple came down the path.

'Hullo.' Annie spoke in her polite voice. Dad always said, 'Talk to the visitors, don't just walk past them as if they didn't exist.'

'Good afternoon.' The woman stared at her. She smelled of sweet perfume.

Annie launched into the Museum Lecture. If she went fast enough, she wouldn't forget anything. 'There were usually twelve families living here, with three or four children each. It was a "fermtoun", a kind of farming commune. People worked together, but each family had a special skill. Like, the weavers lived here, in the Auld Hoose, the family over there in cottage 3 made shoes, the blacksmith was very important – and the two families by the gate did the fishing.'

'Fishing?' the man said.

Annie hurried on. 'Yes. Oh, and, to grow crops the families took turn about at having the good strips of infield land – that means the land here, among the cottages. They shared the outfield, or common-land behind the fermtoun, for their animals' grazing. They didn't *own* their land, but paid a kind of rent, partly money and partly stuff like eggs or grain or cloth, to the laird. He owned the whole of Glenmellish. The children had to help their mothers with the dairying and the poultry and the making of clothes, but in the winter months they had school lessons, in the old barn ...'

She turned round, but the couple had wandered off.

She heard a giggle. Duncan came round the side of the house. 'Talking to yourself is the first sign of madness.'

'You gave me a fright.' Annie was glad enough to have company. She held out her can, 'Drink?' She sat on the bench.

Duncan hirpled over and sat beside her. 'Megabyte's run off again.' He took the can and drank thirstily.

'No,' said Annie.

'She went after a rabbit. Dogs are a pain.'

'Oh, not. She's just following her instincts. Dogs are meant to be hunters, aren't they?'

Duncan shrugged. 'The one thing I'm feared of is she'll get shot for chasing sheep. Old Clerk wouldn't give her a second chance.'

'Murdo's dad?'

'My gran says he's worse than Murdo.'

Annie didn't want to think about Murdo. She wanted to talk about dogs. 'What kind of dog *is* Megabyte?'

'A menace,' said Duncan grimacing.

'No, but really.'

'She's a lurcher.'

Annie giggled. 'Because she lurches about?'

Duncan gave her a shove. 'No. Lurchers are a mixture of a working dog and another breed.'

'Like, a mongrel.'

'Sort of. Like, I think Meg's half collie and half whippet. Gran got her from the rescue kennels in the town.' Duncan looked about. 'Meg just goes. Vanishes. Right now I'd swop her for your green bike.' He pulled a piece of grass and chewed the end. 'Show me where you found your shirt.'

'There, on the wee bridge. Must have been doo-lally.' Annie tried to sound cool. In the bright sunshine everything looked normal. But she still felt spooky when she remembered last night.

For a while neither of them spoke. Duncan began to whistle softly through his teeth, a jaunty fiddle tune. She tried whistling too, but she wasn't much good.

The sun sparkled on the burn, dazzling her for a minute. She noticed that Duncan had gone very still. He was staring at the trunk of the big tree. What was he looking at?

'Duncan, what – ?' She followed his gaze.

Oh! Sunlight dappled down through the branches of the old pine shimmering light and shade over the bridge. There stood the ghost boy, transparent as a cobweb.

As she gazed at him, he became quite real. He wore only ragged trousers, torn off at the knee. His feet were bare and his legs covered in mud. He didn't seem aware of Duncan and Annie at all. Whistling the same tune as them, he up-ended a wooden pail, sat down on it and started sharpening a sickle with a long piece of stone, his red hair flopping over his eyes. Patiently he honed the curved edge, his whetstone making rhythmic rasping sounds. Every now and then he tested the sickle's sharpness with his thumb.

Annie drew in her breath to speak. But Duncan put his hand on her arm and very slightly shook his head. She waited.

A waft of cool air, and the smell of cows and peat-smoke passed across her face, and a woman appeared with a baby wrapped in the folds of her shawl. She too had bare muddy feet. Gently she paddled into the burn, leaning down to clean her legs. Then she spoke: 'Jock, mind Chrissie's bairn for me? It's time I was at the milkin'.'

'Aw, Ma, I've tae cut rushes for faither.' The boy jerked his head towards the boggy ground beyond the burn. 'He's wantin' tae mend the thatch. Why canna Chrissie look efter her own wean?'

A girl came out, plaiting her long tangly red hair. The woman unwound the shawl and laid the baby down on it among the flowers and grasses beside him. It sneezed and waved its feet and arms.

'Chrissie's tae feed the chookie hens, that's why.' The woman ruffled the boy's hair, gave him a little push, and pulled the pail from under him. He rolled on the ground, laughing, 'Och, Ma,' then began to play with the infant.

One of the cows appeared out of the shadows behind the Gallows Tree, mooing gently. The woman called, 'Come on my lass, come here, Blackie.' She sat herself down on an old tree stump. The cow came towards her, she stroked its flank, then leaning her head against it she began to milk.

Annie could hear the rhythmic squirt and splash of the milk as it hit the wooden sides of the pail.

After a while the woman began to talk again. 'We'll be away up to the sheiling when the hill grass has grown

enough. I like that. And your faither's tae rebuild the house this summer. That old wooden lintel's fu' o' rot and I'm no' wantin' the hoose fallin' doon on us wi' the first winter storm.'

The boy sighed.

'Aye, I know, Jock. You'd stay doon here and dae the men's work. Next year. You'll be fourteen then, though I canna believe it.'

A man swung into view, a long scythe over his shoulder.

Jock leaped to his feet. 'Faither!'

The woman gave the cow a last stroke and shoved her away. She picked up the baby and wrapped the shawl around herself, winding the child into its folds.

The man leaned on his scythe. 'They say the young Laird's comin' himsel' tae put us out.'

The woman shook her head. 'Black Alastair. Put us out?' A worried frown crossed her face. 'But they've aye said our glen's no' right for sheep.'

'It's no' for sheep. They say his auld man's bribin' him tae stay here wi' promises o' a deer park.'

'A deer park? Is thore no' plenty deer on the hills?'

The father mimicked a fancy accent, 'Deer is the latest fashion. He wants tae show off to his London friends, take them shootin' and they'll be bound tae catch somethin'. And we're the last faimily in his way.'

The mother said, 'Och, there's nae enduring them. It was sheep they put in Glen Shira in my mother's young days. That's why she brought us here tae Glenmellish.'

'Aye, well they torched anither fermtoun yesterday. The Laird's men did it.'

'What happened tae the folk there?'

The father spat. 'Put intae a ship for the colonies. Given "free passage" – nae choice in the maiter, in ither words.'

Jock snarled, 'If yon Black Alastair comes here I'll see to him.' His sickle flashed in the sunlight as he leaped onto a rock, brandished it and yelled, 'A MacKimbel!'

From the shadows came the sound of barking. A small black dog came frisking through the burn, so that the sunlight splashed rainbows in the spray. Barking joyfully, Megabyte threw herself at Duncan, flinging water everywhere, bouncing all over him and licking his face.

When Annie looked up again, Jock and his family had vanished. All that remained was the dazzle of sunlight on the burn, the dappled shade beneath the old tree and the lightest whisper of wind.

Annie breathed, 'Duncan?'

'What?'

'Did you see them? Who are they?'

'I'm not sure. He – the boy Jock – he was like – real.' He ruffled the dog's head. 'You chased them away, Meg.'

But Megabyte pulled away. Then she was circling the tree hysterically, sniffing and whining around the place where Jock had stood.

* * *

When Duncan went home, Annie was scared to stay any longer around the Auld Hoose. Leaping on to her green bike, she pedalled as fast as she could up the track, homeward.

The kitchen smelled of lovely cooking. 'What's for tea, Dad? I'm starving.'

'My, you're out of breath. What's all the hurry for?'

'Nothing.' Annie plonked herself down on a chair.

Dad lifted a pan lid and stirred gently, sniffing the steam. 'Mmm. I'm doing Mum's favourite, lamb hotpot. The inspectors have been here and she was brilliant. Can you lay the table? Just the three of us – Jo-Ellen's working late again.'

'Nice.' Annie smiled. 'Just us, for once.'

Dad added some herbs. 'Now, make the table look a bit special? Then call Mum. I'm going to pour her a drink.'

Annie chose their best cutlery and found some pretty paper napkins with bluebells on. After furling them into the tumblers, she found Mum standing in the Visitor Centre window gazing out at the elderly couple who were driving out of the gate in an ancient sports car. 'Tea's ready, Mum. What's up?'

'I'm wondering what they really thought,' said Mum.

45

Annie didn't understand. 'Thought?'

'The inspectors.'

'Who? You mean *they* were the inspectors? But you said – '

Mum followed her through to the house. 'I was slopping about – look at me! I thought – och, just another pair of geriatrics looking for something to fill their time – '

Annie sat down. 'Me too. I did the Museum talk. They didn't seem very interested.'

Mum said, 'I'd already done it.'

'Oh no!'

Dad served up steaming platefuls of food. 'Before they left they were *very* complimentary, Moira.'

Mum blushed. 'Well, Keith, people don't always *mean* what they say. Let's wait and see what sort of a rating they actually *give* us – if any.'

* * *

At school, Annie and Sadie worked together, trying to decipher their bit of the parish records. Sometimes the sloping handwriting was hard to read.

Annie nudged Sadie. 'Your family married an awful lot of Clerks. Maybe you'll end up Mrs Murdo Clerk!'

Sadie looked up sideways at her and made a face.

Annie giggled. 'Look at their names – *Mildred* Munro, Bartholomew Clerk and their daughter *Purity*.'

Sadie snorted.

Annie suddenly had an idea. 'Duncan, who's on your sheet?'

He shoved the crumpled photocopy across the table.

Annie turned the pages. 'Maybe the MacKimbels – '

'MacKimbel?' The teacher came over. 'Not, I think, a local

46

name. Maybe you've read it wrongly? Let me see – where is it?'

Annie nudged Duncan.

Duncan blushed scarlet. 'Oh – er – '

The teacher beamed at him. 'Ah – the Worldwide Web, Duncan?'

Duncan smiled uncertainly at her. 'Yes, that's right. The Worldwide Web.' He swallowed. 'I did get a hit last night.'

The teacher brightened. 'Oh?'

'A – Canadian.' Duncan's voice sounded more confident. 'Wanted to know everything I could tell about Glenmellish and – and the MacKimbels.'

'But that's wonderful!' The teacher was ecstatic. 'So, we've found a Glenmellish descendant already. Well done, Duncan. Let's offer to send him all our findings, when our project's complete? Now, would you care to add the name MacKimbel to our Ancestor Tree?'

Duncan smiled shyly and hirpled over to collect a label and a felt pen.

The teacher enthused, 'Annie, search the phone book to see if any MacKimbels still live in this area.'

Annie picked up the heavy directory. She already knew the answer because she'd looked. No MacKimbels would be there. 'Why didn't you tell *me* about your Canadian?' she whispered. But she was feeling relieved. No way could they explain to the teacher that they knew the name MacKimbel only because a ghost boy had shouted it.

She pulled Duncan's copy of the parish register across. Peering once more into the neat handwriting, Annie suddenly let out a yelp. 'Auchentibart! It's here.'

'Quiet, Annie,' called the teacher. 'We're *all* trying to work.'

'Sorry, Miss.' Annie felt elated. There was her home,

written about all these years ago. *Roderick Nic-Caimbeil, weaver, tenant at Auchentibart in 1834.* She was just about to show it to Duncan when the bell rang for the end of lessons.

BLACK ALASTAIR

After tea, Jo-Ellen tackled the washing up. 'I got some noos for you. Like to hear it, eh?'

'Indeed. But you shouldn't be doing this,' said Mum, getting out the Dyson.

'Honey, it's a pleasure,' said Jo-Ellen. 'My research at Ardmellish House is almost done and I feel wunnerful. Now all I need is a liddle sunshine so I can video a few scenes with my camcorder – and I'm done. You've looked after me beaudifully for four weeks. Washing up makes me feel homey. Now, my noos?'

'Oh well, thanks,' said Mum. 'Annie, will you dry? I've got the Visitor Centre to clean. Yes, Jo-Ellen, what news?'

From the basket of dry washing, Annie chose the tea towel with the Dalmatians on it. Underneath lay the old shirt. She stared at it, thinking of Jock. Outside the daylight was fading into grey drizzle.

Jo-Ellen scrubbed at a pot. 'This won't take long, Moira. You were tellin' me about your cash-flow problems? Hope you don't mind, but I mentioned it to Mr Hassan. Did you know his family run a big charitable trust?'

Mum unwound the cable of the vacuum cleaner. 'Must be nice to have money to give away.'

Jo-Ellen went on, 'Part of the trust's aim is to help support local cultural ventures. Mr Hassan thinks this liddle museum is excellent, but lacks focus.'

'Focus?' Mum was obviously interested.

'Mr Hassan says, if you can come up with a really good scheme for marketing the museum, you could apply for this year's award.'

'What sort of scheme?' asked Annie.

Mum said, 'Well, we must be able to think of *something*. What a brilliant opportunity.' She glanced at the clock. 'Can we talk later, while I do the ironing?'

'Sure. But there's no time to lose. The deadline for applications is the end of May. I brought you the form anyway.'

When Mum had gone, Jo-Ellen said, 'Hey, honey, will you miss me?'

Jo-Ellen wasn't that bad and she did know a lot, thought Annie, fighting with the truth for a moment. She *was* looking forward to just being a family again, but you couldn't exactly say that. Partly to avoid answering the question she said, 'Um – something happened yesterday.' She glanced in the direction of the vacuuming noises.

Jo Ellen handed her a dripping plate. 'This has to do with the shirt?'

Annie nearly dropped the plate. 'How did you know?'

'Well go on. I sure knew *something* would happen.' Jo-Ellen's eyes sparkled with curiosity.

But when Annie started talking about seeing the ghost family, before she'd even mentioned Jock, Jo-Ellen interrupted, 'Maybe you saw my ancestor! For goodness sakes, my great-however-many-greats-grandmother might have been there – the girl I've been trying to find out about in all these documents. She must only have been a baby when she, her mother and grandmother were cleared from Auchentibart in 1850 and sent to Nova Scotia.'

'What was her name?'

'That I have failed to find out,' said Jo-Ellen, pulling the plug out and gazing at the dirty water swirling down the drain. 'All I have is this.' She dug in her pocket and produced a scrap of cloth with the letter *C* embroidered on it.

Annie had an idea. 'It's my night to lock up. Why don't you come with me? If we take the shirt, maybe they'll appear again and you could – '

'No, honey. It's no good, eh. I don't have the gift.'

'The gift?'

'Only a few people have the gift, eh. Some can foretell the future, some can delve into people's souls. Others, like you and Duncan, can see – and it seems hear – ghosts. Say, how does it feel?'

'Weird.' Annie dropped the fork she was drying. As she stooped to pick it up, the faintest movement beyond the window caught her eye. It was as if a human shape, slightly darker than the drizzle, moved aside like a net curtain drifting in the wind. 'I don't know if I'd like to see them again.'

Jo-Ellen's beady eyes bored into Annie's. 'Ghosts do often mean trouble.'

'Trouble?'

'When a ghost contacts a living person, it can be a warning of disaster.' Jo-Ellen reached across and gripped Annie's arm. 'The only sure way to stop it is to give back the shirt.

You must take it down to the bridge tonight and leave it there. Don't stop, even if you hear anything.'

Slowly Annie picked up the shirt and hugged it to her chest. Her mind flooded with the memory of Jock and his family, his joy when his father came striding down the path. You couldn't really be afraid of Jock; he was just a boy. There was something about him she'd liked. Perhaps he *would* talk to her, would explain if danger truly threatened her. It was the strange notion of ghosts that frightened her.

'Whatever you do, once you've dropped the shirt do – not – look – back, eh.' Jo-Ellen wagged a bony finger with each word.

Through in the Visitor Centre, the Dyson stopped. In the silence, rain splattered against the window panes, making runnels of water pour down them like tears.

Pushing the shirt into her jacket and grabbing the keys, feeling nervous and excited, Annie said, 'Don't let's bother Mum with this. She's got enough on her mind, okay?'

* * *

Head down into the rain, Annie hurried along, her mind full of questions. Was Jo-Ellen right about the ghost family meaning disaster? Then why had they seemed so happy? What *sort* of disaster could be threatening her? What if she decided not to give back the shirt? Part of her was curious to see what would happen next. Part of her liked the idea of getting to know a boy from the past. And part of her felt scared.

Passing the hen-run she saw the fox prowling along, his reddish-brown fur wet with rain. 'Shooh,' she shouted. 'You're not eating *our* hens. Go away!'

He turned his foxy face to look at her for a moment, his

eyes bright and cheeky, then he turned away, his brushy tail hanging low, merging with the bushes.

She clamped the hen-run padlocks shut thinking, whew, looks like I got here just in time.

One by one she locked up the cottages. She sloshed along the path to the Auld Hoose bridge, the shirt warm inside her jacket. Would Jock appear? Pulling it out, laying it on the bridge, she whispered into the night air, 'We cleaned this for you.'

She'd wait for a minute by the yew tree, before locking up the Auld Hoose. Just in case there was anything to see.

The rain stopped. The moon came out quite suddenly, as if someone had switched on a light. And a shadow was materialising beside the shirt!

Jock was looking straight at her. Suddenly, he picked up the shirt with the pointed end of his sickle and tossed it at her. She tried to dodge sideways, but the sleeves wrapped themselves around her and clung on.

Jock threw his head back and laughed. Waving the sickle at her, he ran up the path and darted in at the Auld Hoose doorway.

Dare she follow him inside? She'd only taken one step when she heard a clinking sound behind her.

Beneath the Gallows Tree the shapes of men on horseback had appeared out of nowhere. The sound was the jingling of their bridles.

One rode forward, swathed in a black cloak, his face hidden under his hat. From the crook of his arm hung a long gun.

Jock's father emerged from the Auld Hoose. He picked up a stone and threw it, yelling something in Gaelic.

Quite casually, the horseman raised the gun. 'Ye shouldnae hae done that. Ye were warned, Roderick MacKimbel. Three times. Ye wouldnae go.'

Bang! Fire spat from the gun. Clouds of smoke from its barrel didn't quite obscure the figure of Jock's father crumpling slowly to the ground.

From the doorway, Jock's mother came running, passing Annie so close she could smell the peat-smoke from the woman's clothes. She bent over her husband, wailing.

Chrissie ran after her, the baby's head bobbing from her shawl. She shouted, 'Alastair, ye promised we could stay till ye'd – ' she tripped and fell. The baby rolled from her shawl, screaming.

Jock's mother looked up. 'Yer weel named, Black Alastair, for every soul in Glenmellish has reason tae hate ye.' She turned, keening, to the body of her husband.

Black Alastair looked up from reloading his gun. 'Here's my last word. The good ship *Atlantis* sails on the morning tide. Chrissie, like I told ye, yer fares are all paid. Be there, or be declared outwyles, the lot of ye, to be hunted high and low. For ye're no longer welcome on my father's lands.'

Jock erupted from the doorway, whirling his sickle round his head. The burnished steel flashed in the moonlight, glinting against the dark sky.

Too late, Black Alastair looked up. He cursed, raised the gun again and spat, 'Drop that, Jock MacKimbel, or you'll be sharing your father's fortunes.'

The mother hurled a stone.

The same instant, Jock threw his sickle. It flew towards the man, an arc of whirling silver.

Whap! Black Alastair's horse reared up, neighing with fright.

Annie heard the thud as he fell. His horse turned and galloped away into the night.

Jock thrust his fist in the air and yelled, 'A MacKimbel!'

The mother cried, 'Jock, get away, lad. Dinnae let them catch ye!'

For a single still moment Jock's eyes met Annie's, fox's eyes full of defiance, before he sprinted away, vanishing into the woods.

Under the tree, men were leaping from their horses. Some went after Jock. Annie could hear them crashing through the woods. Another ran into the house. He emerged brandishing a burning log from the fire. As he passed Annie, a piece fell off. She felt the heat of it scald the skin of her leg, heard it sizzle on her boot as she kicked it away. The smoke made her cough.

Cursing as an ember scorched his hand, the man flung the log up onto the thatch, crackling and sparking. Soon clouds of smoke swirled around, followed by tongues of flame.

The last thing Annie saw in the glare of the fire was the men crowding round the mother, Chrissie and the crying infant, roping them together.

Two terrified cows charged out from the doorway just as the roof crashed in. Flames crackled up, roaring into the night sky, blinding Annie.

She fled. Running as fast as she could, expecting to hear the crack of gunfire, to feel the bullet hit her, she leaped the bridge.

Now there was silence. The moon was gazing down

placidly on Auchentibart Museum of Country Life and all who lived there, for all the world as if nothing at all had happened.

Annie's heart was still pounding when she clicked open the latch of the kitchen door.

'Wellies off,' came Mum's voice. 'Okay?'

Kicking off her boots, still shaking with fright, Annie tried to catch her breath before she went into the kitchen.

Mum looked up from the tapestry she was framing. 'Hi, love. How about a hot bath?'

It was all Annie could do not to burst into tears. She lay soaking in warm water, coloured green with Mum's best pine bath oil, mulling over what she'd seen. Could she have imagined it all?

Afterwards, wrapped in Dad's thick blue bathrobe, she sat sipping hot chocolate in the kitchen.

Dad clattered in. 'What the blinking blazes happened to this?' He came into the kitchen holding up Annie's welly.

A weal of melted plastic split into a gaping hole, like a horrible smile, right across the toe.

All weekend the sun shone. A steady trickle of visitors wandered through the Museum. Jo-Ellen seemed to be everywhere, filming with her little silver camcorder. Mum demonstrated wool-spinning, Dad manned the till and they both sold entry tickets and souvenirs and handed out information leaflets for people to take round the cottages with them.

Annie helped, serving coffees and ice creams in the Visitor Centre, refilling baskets of shortbread and wiping tables. But all the time, images of fire kept flaring up in her mind. Questions followed each other – the dreadful scene she'd witnessed at the Auld Hoose – what did it mean? More importantly, had Jock got away – or had he been caught?

In the evening, Mum asked, 'What's up, Annie? You've hardly said a word all day.'

But Annie's thoughts were still too confused to be explained. 'Nothing,' she said.

Mum looked at Dad. 'Let's do something different tonight.'

Dad agreed, 'Okay. It's been a better day.'

'We should celebrate,' said Mum. 'Let's make a time capsule.'

'Good idea,' said Dad. 'And I've got just the right container.' He went out.

Annie was mildly interested. 'What's a time capsule?'

'You package together a few things about your life and times, and bury them.'

'Like, where?'

Dad came back in with her holey welly. 'This'll do for a container. Now, what are we going to put in? Let's see. Some of your blue wool, Moira? One of our publicity leaflets? A crisp packet?'

'Yes,' said Mum, 'And a pound note. Annie, you write

down all our names and ages and the date. Use indelible pen, mind.' Soon they had the welly stuffed with little objects.

Annie had an idea. 'We could put in that old shirt.' For now she couldn't wait to get rid of it.

'Too big,' said Dad. 'Anyway, what's it got to do with our lives?'

Annie wrote their names and dates, but added her own private note, *We are not the only family at Auchentibart. There's the MacKimbels. They lived here long ago, but their ghosts are still around, I don't know why. I want to stay here and we only have three weeks to think up a good idea so's we win the Trust money.*

'Now,' said Mum. 'Where are we going to bury our time capsule? It's got to be well hidden, so no one will find it for – oh, a hundred years.'

After a little argument they decided to lever up the loose bottom step below the back door and put it there. Dad used ready-mixed concrete to seal it in – and stuck the step down properly on top of it. 'This'll take some finding,' he said with satisfaction.

Somehow Annie felt better afterwards. She'd written down what was birling round her head – about the ghosts. And buried it.

* * *

One morning, when Annie opened her curtains, a big grey cloud filled the sky, with a rainbow in front. She ran to the back door shouting, 'Look,' and nearly crashed into Jo-Ellen.

The rainbow arched over the whole Museum, making a frame for all the cottages, so bright that it even had a faint shadow of itself above.

'Hmm, a *frostic*,' said Jo-Ellen, aiming her camcorder at the sky.

'*Frostic*?' Annie said.

'Yes. Ancient Norse peoples believed that a *frostic* – a rainbow – was their bridge to heaven; when they died their souls would cross the rainbow to meet up with the souls of their dead friends.'

Annie quite liked this thought.

Jo-Ellen stopped filming. 'Want a lift to school today? I've a date at the library to look at an old journal they've dug up.'

Anything was better than the school bus. Annie said, 'Okay. Um – what's a journal?'

'A diary, but filled with your thoughts about things that happen, not just dental appointments and birthdays. I might give you one for your birthday. When is it?'

'28th May.'

'Right. That's about the deadline for the Hassan Trust, eh? Anyway, the librarian says she has found the journal of a minister who looked after this parish in the mid 1800s.'

Immediately, Annie was interested. 'Could I borrow it?'

'Doubtful. It's very fragile. They had to get special permission from HQ for me to handle it.'

Annie began putting out the breakfast things, humming absent-mindedly. Jo-Ellen began singing along with her, '*Fosgail an doras dhan tàillear fhìdhlear, Fosgail an doras dhan fhìdhlear thàilleir.*' At the end she said, 'Boy, that crazy liddle song goes back a long way.'

How could Jo-Ellen know this? 'That's Duncan's tune.' Annie felt weird again. 'Haven't a clue what the words mean.'

'Cheery, eh? "Open the door for the fiddling tailor, Open the door for the tailoring fiddler." My mother used to sing me to sleep, singing it, when I was a liddle girl.'

'You know lots of old stuff,' said Annie. 'Is it true people got chased out of their houses just to make room for animals?'

Jo-Ellen glanced sharply at her. 'Have you seen – something more?'

But Annie burst into tears. She couldn't bear to remember the events of that dreadful night down at the Auld Hoose.

Jo-Ellen patted her roughly on the shoulder. 'Sorry to upset you, eh? I can't help wanting to know more, you know? Yes, some of the landowners really did evict their tenants. You see, in these days the poor tenants had no rights.'

Dad came through with the mail.

Mum swept in. 'Coffee, Jo-Ellen?'

Once the fragrant aroma of coffee was wafting about, Mum said, 'Next Sunday's our Gala Day. It's a good old Museum tradition and all the oldies in the Glen come along – you'll love to hear their stories, Jo-Ellen.'

'Fine, honey. And I'm hoping my brother Mack will be here in time – he's coming to pick me up and we're going to do a liddle travelling together before going home, eh.'

Dad sorted letters into brown and white piles. 'Nothing for you, Moira.' He slit open a white one.

Annie saw his face go serious. 'What is it?'

'The school I applied to. They say there won't be any work for me there this year.' He blew out a great gusty sigh.

'Oh no,' said Mum.

'Oh yes,' Dad cleared his throat noisily. 'So – I'll just – er – go and finish up in the Visitor Centre.'

Relief washed through Annie. For the time being she was safe, she could stay here, though she felt sorry he was disappointed.

Mum glanced at the clock. 'Annie, look at the time. Off you go.'

Jo-Ellen said, 'I'm giving her a lift today.'

They drove along in silence for a while, then Jo-Ellen said, 'You put back the shirt?'

Feeling awkward, Annie confessed, 'I – I tried. But he – the boy threw it back at me.'

'I see.' Jo-Ellen sniffed. 'Well, I hope very much you're not now in some real danger, eh.'

ACCIDENT

High on the cold and windy hillside, the Clerk's farm crouched like an old grey sheep, bedraggled and unloved. In the rain-swept yard, a thin collie howled on the end of a chain, her tail between her legs, a puppy wriggling beneath her.

Murdo stood in front of her protectively, clutching his ear. It hurt badly. Even school would be better than this. Rain ran down the back of his neck. It dripped off his nose like tears. He'd managed to keep the pup hidden till this morning.

His father glared at him. 'That'll teach ye a lesson.' He rubbed his knuckles together. 'I tellt ye tae drown the pups.'

Murdo yelled, 'Ye kicked Bess that bad they were a' born deid but this yin.'

'Och, Bess is past it. I'm away for the shotgun.'

At the sound of her name, the dog wagged her tail, looking up at Murdo with trust in her eyes.

Murdo shouted, 'Ye'll no' harm Bess. She's – she wis Ma's dug. If Ma wis here ye'd never dare.'

'Well, "Ma" isnae here. Ach, ye'r saft in the heid. Ye were aye a right mammy's boy.'

Murdo felt sick. He would never forget the long coffin, the white flowers.

Bess licked his hand as though she could read his mind. 'Quiet, lass,' he said.

His father ranted, 'Get rid o' that dog before I come hame. If it cannae work it cannae eat.' He spat, 'And I didnae keep ye aff the school to staun aboot like a wiltin' leek.' He clambered in to a rusting tractor. 'Yon slurry wilnae spread itsel'.' The tractor rattled away, its muck-spreader swinging crazily, flinging clods of mud from its wheels.

Murdo watched him go, black hatred in his heart. The folk who watched his father hand out the hymn books in the kirk on Sundays, all dressed up in the square-shouldered suit, with his hair greased back, they had no idea what he was really like. The Bible said you had to love your father. He couldn't.

Bess whimpered. She was his last link with Ma, who'd trained her up to be such a great sheepdog. Where could he hide her and the pup safely? Miserably, he stood stroking her ear, trying to think, his head throbbing with pain from where his father had slugged him. In the distance, the tractor grumbled down the farm track to the field. And slowly an idea began to grow in his mind.

* * *

Annie was first to arrive at school. She sat on the playground wall thinking, why am *I* having all this trouble? Why's Jock hassling *me*, not someone else? What am I meant to *do*?

The sun glimmered on the sea. Far away, a thin youth wandered along the beach, trailing a stick, head down.

Sss-s-ss! The school bus drew up in front of her, hissing its brakes and giving her a fright. Her friends leaped onto the pavement, chattering and laughing.

Sadie was breathless. 'Murdo missed the bus.' She stuck her tongue out at her brother Coll as it drove away. He made a face back at her through the window, then waved.

Duncan hirpled along with them, 'Maybe Murdo's old man chained him up.'

Annie and Sadie snorted with laughter and made Murdo-like grunts and growls.

In school, Mrs McCrindle pinned a huge map on the wall. 'Some early Scots emigrants named their new bit of Canadian land Nova Scotia. It means New Scotland.'

Annie said, 'Our lodger comes from Nova Scotia.'

Mrs McCrindle beamed at her. 'Many families from Glenmellish were cleared from their homes after the 1745 rebellion. Most were sent across the Atlantic. As you know, we've found descendants of Munros, Clerks and Macintyres, and Duncan is searching the Worldwide Web for more.'

As the teacher talked on about Glenmellish emigrants, Annie gazed out of the window at the sea. She tried to imagine the people who Black Alastair had sent away on 'the good ship *Atlantis*' from Ardmellish so long ago. Had they been scared? Had they been excited like she'd been at the thought of coming here? Had they been sad to leave their beloved homes, like the desperate refugees you saw on telly?

The youth she'd seen on the beach was now sitting on the playground wall, looking out to sea. She could see his knobbly backbone.

By midday, he'd gone. After school, Annie went home with Sadie, to watch *Neighbours* and have tea. Later, she was to cycle home. Mum was away to the town.

Going along the track to the house, Sadie picked a handful

of bluebells. She turned her eyes on Annie, 'I've a great idea – aboot yon Murdo.' She burst into giggles.

'What?'

'Oh, oh, I cannae speak – ' Sadie clutched her sides, laughing till she fell over.

'Sadie!'

'Daddy was guttin' fish. I got a wee bag o' fishguts off him. For tae – um – perfume big Murdo's PE bag.'

Annie started to laugh. Then she got worried. 'But how –?'

'Och, no problem. On the bus. You'll can distract him.' Sadie fell about. 'When he opens his bag his kit'll be mingin'.'

Annie said, 'He'll kill you!'

But Sadie was dancing away up the track, chanting 'Mingin' Murdo' at the top of her voice.

The cottage was small and cosy and rather dark inside. The old dog, Bracken, lay by the empty fireplace. She thumped her tail on the floor when Sadie bounced in, followed by Annie.

Sadie stuck her bluebells in a jam jar of water, switched on the TV and lay down on the floor, her head on Bracken's side. She began flicking through channels with the remote control.

Up till now, Annie had said nothing to Sadie about Jock.

Mr Munro came in with a mug of tea. 'Would youse like a piece and jam?'

Sadie nodded vigorously, her eyes on the screen.

While he was busy making their sandwiches, Annie said, 'Sadie?'

'Aye?'

'It's about, um, this sort of boy I've been seeing.'

Sadie goggled at her. '*Sort* of boy?'

'Well, it's – he's a ghost.'

Sadie's voice was full of exaggerated horror. 'Oh my.'

Annie persevered. She told Sadie everything she'd seen. But Sadie wouldn't take her seriously and was still giggling and making spooky noises when Mr Munro returned. He always filled sandwiches generously and soon Sadie's mouth was full and her face liberally smeared with raspberry jam.

After tea, Annie headed homewards on her green bike. She and Sadie often biked between each other's houses if nobody was giving them a lift. It was a sunny evening and she'd be home in time to help Dad.

Sadie's track was bumpy and you had to avoid the worst potholes, but Annie reached the main road safely and began cycling up the hill. Usually she had to get off and walk the last bit, but tonight she stood on the pedals, determined to keep going to the top. Puffing, she made it, her legs aching. Great! She could freewheel all the way down to the Museum. She whizzed along. There were the cottages. One corner to negotiate, past the wee wood and she'd be home.

With a roar, a huge lorry laden with tree trunks came hurtling round the corner. She wobbled. Oh no! Her front wheel hit a stone at the edge of the road. Crash! Annie flew headlong into the ditch. It was full of prickly brambles. The lorry rattled away up the hill, leaving only the smells of pine resin and diesel. Had the driver not seen her?

She lay in the soggy ditch, dizzy with pain. Oh, her knee hurt. She cried for a minute, feeling alone.

But eventually she managed to pick herself up. Blood streamed down her leg from the gash on her knee. Her arms were all scraped and scratched and her face felt sticky, as her tears dried.

A whiff of cool air, and Jock stood beside her, hands on hips, looking down at her. He shook his head slowly, smiling. He'd better not be laughing at her.

He beckoned and she limped after him, as if in a dream. He led her along the ditch, over the wall and down through the wood to a little dell, green with moss. There, a spring bubbled out of the ground, surrounded by grass that looked like fine green hair, scattered with primroses and violets. Small spiders' webs rested on the grass like silvery nets.

Annie sat down. By now the blood from her knee had dripped down to her sock.

Jock pulled a handful of sphagnum moss, dipped it in the spring and began washing all the scratches on her arms and legs, last of all her knee.

Annie watched his face as he worked. He looked so thin and pale you could almost see through to his bones.

With great care, he lifted one of the spider's webs and laid it over her wound. On top he placed a fresh pad of sphagnum moss. Pulling a length of rough string from his pocket, he bound it neatly.

Annie was so amazed by the whole thing, still shocked from her fall, that she hadn't uttered a word. Now she said, 'Thanks.'

He looked into her eyes for a moment, but said nothing. Cupping his hands, he filled them with spring water and made her drink some. It tasted sparklingly fresh.

She felt better. The worst of the pain in her knee was wearing off. A thought came into her mind; had the boy on the beach this morning been Jock?

As if he could read her mind, he smiled mischievously.

Annie blurted out, 'Is it true you're warning me about some disaster?'

Jock's expression changed. He looked anxious for a moment. Suddenly he bent and picked three violets. He stuck them in her moss bandage. He stood back, hands on hips, laughing.

He was as changeable as the weather, thought Annie, looking down at her flowery bandage.

When she looked up he'd gone.

She waited for ages, but he didn't come back. The pain ebbed away from her knee and slowly she clambered back up to the road. Luckily her bike was okay. Deep in thought, she cycled slowly home.

She was in the kitchen peeling a banana when Jo-Ellen came in.

'Whut's that?' Jo-Ellen pointed a bony finger at Annie's knee. 'Did you kneel on a bird's nest?'

Annie told her what had happened.

'Magic. But this ghost boy's far too friendly. You must be careful.'

Annie shrugged.

Jo-Ellen bent to examine the bandage. 'Sphagnum moss, eh? A natural antiseptic. And gypsies used spiders' webs to heal cuts on their horses' legs. Something in the web helps blood coagulate. Oh, he's tied it all together with nettle-stem cord!' She started making coffee. 'Nettle leaves make great soup, and the stems have this useful fibre.'

Annie said, 'How'm I supposed to know what he wants, if he won't speak to me?'

The rising steam hid the old woman's expression. She seemed to be staring right through Annie to somewhere beyond. 'He could be wanting his freedom.'

'Freedom?'

'There must be some reason he can't rest at peace. Perhaps he believes only you can free his spirit.'

'How would I know how to do that?'

Jo-Ellen spoke softly, 'I've read about hauntings and there's always something – some reason the person's spirit can't leave the place. Perhaps this boy committed a crime, perhaps he lost someone dear to him here, perhaps nobody mourned for him when he died. Who knows?'

It was a relief to be talking about Jock. A crime? Jock had thrown his sickle at Black Alastair. Had it killed him? But no, she couldn't bear to conjure it all up again. She was too frightened. She'd done her best to forget the terrifying scene of Jock's family being cleared from the Auld Hoose, so that now she was beginning to wonder if she could have dreamed up the nightmare herself. Yet an hour ago, Jock had seemed real enough. To divert the confusion of her thoughts, she said, 'How could I find out what he wants?'

Jo-Ellen sipped her coffee in silence for a minute. 'Maybe your mate Duncan could help, eh. He's seen him too, so you're in this together, whatever it is.'

'Okay.' The prospect of Duncan helping made Annie feel lots better. Duncan was clever. She finished her banana. She'd phone him later.

Jo-Ellen pulled some paper from her briefcase. 'Oh, and maybe there's a clue in this lot. I photocopied a couple of pages from the minister's journal. I thought they might interest you. Did I tell you my ancestor was a MacKimbel? We still use the name. My brother Mack, eh? Why, he's J. *MacKimbel* Harrison.'

'MacKimbel!' Annie's heart missed a beat. 'How amazing! That's Jock's name. Why didn't you say?'

'Jock's name?' Jo-Ellen handed her the pages. 'Why didn't *you* say? I've been hunting for any reference to a girl called C. MacKimbel. But I learned quite a lot from your experiences, eh? Helped me look for the right papers in the Hassan archive.'

Annie was speechless. She looked at the copperplate writing.

Jo-Ellen's fingernail pointed to the words *Nic-Caimbeil*. 'Look, here's a MacKimbel. Gaelic spelling, eh?'

'Oh yes,' breathed Annie. 'I saw *Nic-Caimbeil* in the parish register at school, spelled like that. I didn't know –'

Jo-Ellen went on, 'It seems your "Black Alastair" and his family owned all the land hereabouts. His father, Lord Mellish, had arranged for Alastair to marry the wealthy widow of a neighbouring landowner. But Alastair kept putting it off.

* * *

The phone rang. It was Duncan. 'Guess who I met tonight?'

Why did her friends have to play guessing games? Annie said through gritted teeth, 'The cast of *Neighbours*?'

'Oh dear,' said Duncan. 'We are in a bad mood.'

'Sorry,' said Annie. 'Listen, I wanted to talk to you. About Jock?'

'That's what I was *telling* you,' said Duncan. 'I met him. Gran was doing a gig in the hotel. I'd gone to fish off the pier. At first I thought he was a homeless guy, wandering about the harbour. Well, I suppose he is homeless, in a way.'

'Did he talk?'

'Yes. The thing is, he sort of whispers, and sometimes in Gaelic. He wanted to know if your knee was okay. Said he found you in a ditch. What happened?'

Annie explained about the lorry, and falling off.

Duncan went on, 'I tried asking him, you know, why he's around?'

'And he said?' Annie was excited. Now all would be made clear, at last.

'He said he wanted to find out what had happened to his mother and sister. They'd gone away on a boat. Did I know if they had come back? I said sorry, I hadn't a clue. He said – '

Just at that moment, Dad picked up the phone in the Visitor Centre. His voice crackled in her earpiece, 'Annie, I need to use the phone now. You have three seconds to say goodbye.' His receiver clicked off.

'Quick, Duncan, what else?'

'Annie, he seems to think he killed someone and is being hunted by "the Duke's men". D'you think *he* killed Black Alastair?'

Dad chose that moment to disconnect them. The phone went dead.

GALA DAY

Annie thought over that terrifying scene at the Auld Hoose. She tried to recall everything in detail, from the gunning down of Jock's father to Jock hurling the sickle, but she failed. Most of it was lost in a cloud of fear. Could Jock's sickle have killed Black Alastair? She wasn't sure.

One thing she knew. She really wanted to meet up with Jock again. It would be so great to talk with him, to understand more about him. She'd always thought ghosts would be scary, but Jock was different. It was nice knowing he was around, and might appear when you least expected it.

She picked up the pages of the minister's journal. *Buried the last of the MacKimbels today, in our wee graveyard to the back of farmer Clerk's lands in Auchentibart woods. The puir laddie could not have been more than fifteen years of age. I mind giving him a bowl of porridge and a sup of milk if I could catch him, but he'd run away if anyone else came near, wily as a fox, that one, but has sadly now succumbed to starvation, a vagrant. Mony a prayer have I said for his soul, and trust that he may have found his loved ones in Heaven, for there is not one MacKimbel left in Glen Mellish. I paid two shilling to the mason for his name on a tombstone, that this family be not forgotten. And the Almighty bears witness that, although young Jock be in a Better Place than this, I did shed a few tears over his grave.*

* * *

Gala Day at Glenmellish Museum dawned bright and sunny. Dad opened the gates early to let in the first carload of helpers. 'It's looking hopeful,' he said, preparing to sell the first tickets in the Visitor Centre. A special bus had been laid on for the day, to ply between Ardmellish Pier and the Museum.

Mum looked funny in her mob-cap and apron and her long traily skirt, bustling about between the cottages with baskets of supplies.

Almost everyone they knew had come to help. Mrs McCrindle, who was a keen salmon fisher, had brought a selection of rods and was giving casting lessons. Sadie's big brother Coll and his friends came dressed in the farm gear of a hundred years ago. They demonstrated crafts they'd been learning after school like dry-stane dyking and horn carving. The mums cooked puddings and scones and oatcakes over open fires in the cottages.

Annie giggled as she and Sadie put on their white bonnets, blouses and ankle-length skirts, 'We look like giant babies.'

Sadie stuck her tongue out. 'You do.' She looked in the mirror. 'I look real old-fashioned.' She screwed some more of her hair into an elastic band and stuffed it into the cap, which hung all squint. 'Is that awright?'

Annie straightened it for her. 'You'll do.' Sometimes she felt as if she was Sadie's mum. 'D'you think we look authentic?'

'Eh?'

'You know, like people really looked a hundred years ago? I mean, like we were the ghosts of the people who once lived here?' A shiver went up her spine at the thought.

'Och, you and your ghosties,' Sadie rolled her eyes derisively.

By midday the sun was burning down and the tourist carpark was full. The smell of baking was everywhere and people were trying all the different foods. A few thunderclouds began to gather far away to the south, above the hilltops. Sadie's mum and dad arrived on the special bus from the old folk's home. They were wearing their best clothes and hanging on to Sadie's great-granny.

Annie and Sadie were in the Auld Hoose. They were demonstrating how to use a spinning wheel to make yarn.

Outside, by the haystack, an elderly shearer called Tam sat on a long wooden stool puffing his pipe and chatting to the visitors. From time to time he would turn a sheep onto its back, heave it onto the stool and hand-cut its fleece off so close you could see its pink skin. Each fleece came off like one big thick jersey, which got rolled up and stuffed into a sack. Sadie's great-granny sat on a straw bale beside him, chatting away.

'Tam and ma great-granny is old pals,' said Sadie, during a lull in the tourists. 'Haw, what's that niff?'

Annie pointed to beyond the Museum grounds. 'Murdo's muck-spreader. Yeuch.'

It was true. Murdo was driving the tractor and making his trailer squirt the most evil-smelling slurry over the field. Some of it was even splattering the cars at the edge of the carpark. As he passed, she could see him grinning.

'He's trying to spoil our Gala Day, that's what he's doing.' Annie was furious.

'Wasn't it no' great, me plankin' the fish guts in his bag?'

Sadie stuck her tongue out at him.

'I thought he was going to molecate the two of us,' giggled Annie.

'Lucky Coll was there. He saved us. "You can have my kit the day," says he tae Murdo. Crawler.'

Mum brought hunks of fleece inside to card and comb into little rolls of fluff ready for the girls to spin. Sadie was doing the spinning because her fingers were nimble and she'd spent the winter practising. Annie did the commentary.

Soon Sadie got up. 'It's your turn tae spin.'

'Only if you'll do the talking.' Annie sat at the wheel. It was difficult to co-ordinate a foot-treadle and think about what your fingers were doing at the same time. The wool felt nice, soft and slightly oily. She tried not to make the yarn too lumpy.

Jo-Ellen came in with a tall man. 'Why look, a spinning wheel, eh?' She zoomed in on Annie's hands with her camcorder.

Sadie wiped her nose on her sleeve, took a deep breath and began in her sing-song school voice, 'First the wool is carded, then the spinner takes a little in her palm, and adds it gradually to the yarn …' She kept going to the end, sniffed loudly and sat down.

'Very interesting,' said the man, laughing a little. 'Thank you both.'

Jo-Ellen fingered the wool coming through Annie's fingers. 'Mmm, it's rougher than you'd think.'

Thanks, thought Annie. I'm only doing my best.

More tourists crammed in to watch and the girls were busy for the next hour.

By the time they stopped it was mid-afternoon. Outside, the air had gone still and heavy. Big purple thunderclouds hung overhead. Annie ran up to the Visitor Centre, as the

rain came on silently at first, then rattling on the roofs. Brightly coloured umbrellas opened all around the Museum like flowers blooming.

Duncan was now indoors, too, playing his fiddle, busking for money, his fiddle case open, with a few coins lying in it. Megabyte sat at his feet, her mouth twitching when he squeaked a high note.

Annie smiled. 'She looks as if she's going to sing.'

Megabyte put her nose in the air and gave a long high howl. Everyone collapsed with laughter, and out of the corner of her eye, Annie glimpsed Jock leaning against the doorway, laughing gleefully too.

Jo-Ellen appeared, filming. 'Mack, turn around and look

intelligent. Meet my landlady's daughter, Annie.'

The man shot his hand out and shook hers vigorously. 'Hi there. Pleased to meet you. Mack Harrison. Say, this young fiddler's not bad, and isn't the dawg terrific?'

Rain dripped from his grey hair, but Annie thought he looked okay.

He grinned, showing a row of large white teeth. 'Did Jo-Ellen mention that we're looking for a location for our next film? We've visited two Clan Centres, but they were awful like theme parks, tartan tour buses and all. Your liddle place here is beaudiful. Where may I find your father, eh?'

'That's him,' Annie pointed. 'At the till.' She knew what Dad's response would be. He couldn't stand TV crews; 'Waste of space, wanting this and that all the time,' he'd be saying, 'and then it's no thanks.'

Jock now hovered around Duncan, dancing a kind of airy jig. It didn't seem as if anyone else could see him. Jo-Ellen kept her camcorder trained on Duncan.

The old shepherd, Tam, came in, wiping his brow. He chose a can from the fridge and chatted to Jock in Gaelic, just as if he was a normal boy. Clearly, Tam could see him. Later, when the rain went off, Jock followed him outside. Annie went too. Hot-Pot was last in the queue for shearing. Jock sat on the fence as Tam rolled her onto her back and started work. The shears looked like two black knives held together with a piece of curved steel.

Jo-Ellen passed with a suitcase. 'Be sure to let me know if you learn anything new about the MacKimbels, Annie. I'm leaving now. Mack's driving me to the airport.'

Annie said, 'Do you need help with your stuff?'

Jo-Ellen said, 'It's all in, thanks, honey. I've had such a marvellous time. I found most of what I came for, bar one, eh.'

'Oh?' Annie looked at her.

'I never found the MacKimbel graveyard. *Auchentibart Woods, at the back of farmer Clerk's land*, wrote the minister. But there's no old woodland, only a horrible block of modern forestry. You can't see a thing through it.'

Sadie wandered along eating crisps.

Jo-Ellen said, 'Annie, don't forget you've only two weeks left to come up with some bright idea to apply for that Trust money.'

Annie said, 'Dad and Mum have been too busy, with Gala Day and things.'

Jo-Ellen waved. 'I know. But there's no time to lose now. Byee.'

Annie smiled and waved vaguely, thinking of the idea which had arrived in her mind an hour ago, but which she didn't feel the need to discuss with anyone quite yet.

After Jo-Ellen and Mack had driven away, Sadie said, 'My Dad showed me an old graveyard up at Clerk's once. It was all hidden away behind a mossy wall.'

Late that night, Annie came into the kitchen after her bath. Her parents sat at the table. They looked done in, she thought.

'You were a real help today, Annie,' said Dad. 'Thanks.'

Annie felt warm inside. 'Did we make enough money?'

Mum smiled. 'We did very well. And what about Mack Harrison, big chief film maker?'

'Big talker,' said Dad.

Mum said, 'Wouldn't it be great if they did choose us for their location? If their film did well, well, think how much good the publicity could do us.'

'Except that we won't be here,' muttered Annie, bitterly.

Somewhere beyond the window, lightning flashed and flickered.

'One, two, three,' she counted, before the thunder came, bumping and rolling so the roof rattled. 'Three miles away – '

'And getting closer.' Dad got up and collected his bundle of keys. 'Just listen to that rain. I'll lock up tonight. You two look tired out.'

'Won't you wait till it passes?' Mum sounded uneasy.

'I'll be fine.' Dad opened the back door. 'Back in ten.' He disappeared into the deluge.

Unlike her mother, Annie wasn't particularly scared of thunderstorms. To take Mum's mind off the din outside, she said, 'Why don't you open your letter?' But when she lifted the letter down from the dresser she wished she'd kept her mouth shut. On it was a blurred stamp that ended, "Education Authority".

Mum, her face white and tense, tore open the envelope with shaking hands. She read for a moment in silence.

Annie watched her expression change.

Mum looked at her. 'They want to interview me for a teaching job.'

Beyond the window, lightning streaked a line of quicksilver across the night sky. It seemed to hover, quivering with electric energy, before zooming earthwards. Bang! Before she had time to begin counting, the explosion shook her house to its foundations. But it wasn't her house that had been struck.

LIGHTNING STRIKE

Annie sat bolt upright. 'That was so near!'

'Hope it wasn't one of the cottages.' Mum's voice wobbled a little. Wearily she covered her face with her hands. 'I don't know what to do about this job.'

'D'you want to be a school teacher again, Mum?'

'No way. I suppose it's the *sensible* thing to do, but – '

Annie's mind was a muddle of feelings and thoughts she couldn't sort out.

The thunderstorm was moving away now, rumbling round the distant hills and the pattering of rain on the window had stopped.

Mum got up. 'What on earth can Dad be doing? "Ten minutes," he said. It's almost midnight, Annie. He's been out for over an hour.'

Just then, Dad clumped in at the back door, dripping wet. 'Did you hear that thunderclap?' He grabbed the green dishtowel and started rubbing his face and hair dry.

'We were just about to send out a search party,' said Mum, helping him peel off his wet jacket.

'What happened?' asked Annie.

Dad leaned against the cooker. Pools of water dripped from his jeans, making a puddle on the floor. The sodden towel wrapped round his head made him look like a surprised cabbage. 'Well, I got as far as the Auld Hoose. The rain was bucketing down. Couldn't find the key. I sheltered under the Gallows Tree for a minute while I fished all the keys out, to find the right one. Then – ' His eyes had a perplexed look in them. 'Then someone – I don't know who, grabbed me and pulled me out.'

Mum said, 'Who on earth would be there at this time of night?'

'I haven't the remotest idea,' said Dad. 'Maybe a tinker lad? Anyway that boy saved my life. That thunderclap? I'll never forget it. A bolt of lightning struck the tree! I'd have been struck too, fried to a crisp, if he hadn't pulled me away.'

'That boy,' thought Annie. Not a tinker lad at all. She knew, without the slightest doubt, that Jock had saved her father's life. Was this the disaster he'd been trying to warn her about?

Dad went on, 'You should have seen it. The whole tree alight with electricity. And the smell – like sulphur, rotten eggs, and hot resin from the burnt wood.'

Mum's face was ashen. 'Oh, Keith, thank goodness you're all right.'

Annie asked eagerly, 'The boy who saved you – what was he like?'

'Well, here's the strange thing,' Dad said. 'I only got a

glimpse of his face. The lighting blinded me for a moment. Afterwards I couldn't find him. I wanted to thank him, bring him back here for a drink or something.' He gazed out of the window. 'The lad looked half-starved.'

Out of the corner of her eye, Annie saw what might have been a trail of mist passing the window. Poor Jock, all alone. She got up and went to the back door. Outside, everything was dark and still. Although she could see nothing, she sensed his presence. '*Tapadh leat*, thanks,' she breathed the only Gaelic she knew into the night. Gently, she shut the door again, thinking how awful it would have been if Dad had been hurt. He was the best Dad in the world and she couldn't imagine life without him.

In the morning, frantic bleating outside her window woke Annie. Nine-thirty, said her clock. Oh no, she'd missed the school bus by more than an hour.

She banged on Mum and Dad's door, 'We've slept in, we're due to open *now*. Something's wrong with Hot-Pot. I'm going to see.' Throwing a jacket over her pyjamas, grabbing the cottage keys, she headed out.

The baaing sounds led her towards the henhouse. At first she thought Hot-Pot had just got herself tangled in the fence. 'Stay still, Hot-Pot. Poor sheep. It's all right, steady girl,' she cooed, trying to calm the wriggling sheep. But as she knelt to free Hot-Pot from the tangle of barbed wire, a scene of utter devastation met her eyes. Black feathers, blood and dead hens were strewn among the grass. A massacre had taken place.

Annie felt horrified and angry. Who had dared to hurt the poor hens? The vandals who'd been harassing Glenmellish for months? Oh, if she could get her hands on them –

'It was the fox.' Jock stood there amongst the carnage.

'The fox?' said Annie, delighted and amazed that Jock had

spoken directly to her for the first time. 'How – ?'

At that moment, Hot-Pot struggled free. She bleated once and trotted off. Somewhere far away a vixen barked. It sounded like a hoarse laugh.

Picking her way through the carcasses, Annie went into the henhouse. Five eggs lay in the nesting boxes, two of them still warm. She turned away with tears in her eyes.

Jock drifted alongside her, appearing and disappearing so that she wondered if he was really there, so thin it looked as if his clothes were worn by sticks instead of legs and arms, like a flimsy scarecrow.

She trudged onward down the path, unlocking the cottages. She felt awful. 'The poor hens,' she said. 'How did the fox got in? Dad was locking up last night and no *way* would he have forgotten the hen-pen.' She began to feel better, talking to Jock.

When they reached the Auld Hoose, she sat down on a stone. The May morning was quiet and calm, washed clean after last night's storm. A robin flew down and perched on the yew tree, cocking his head and chirrupping. It seemed the most natural thing in the world for her to ask, 'Was it true, what happened to you, that night?'

'Yon nicht when Black Alastair killed ma faither?' He looked up, eyes blazing as if he could see it all again.

'Yes,' whispered Annie, afraid to break the spell. 'And you ran away.'

'I went up a tree. I saw them take mother awa'. When they'd a' gone, I came back. They'd left ma faither deid. I got the spade and dug a hole in the ground. Faither wis that heavy, but I managed tae bury him.' Jock wiped his eyes roughly with his knuckles.

Annie felt so sad for him.

Jock said, 'A few days later the men cam' back. They sent

the hounds efter me, but I jumped intae the burn tae throw them off the scent. I paiddled a' the wey up tae yon wee spring.' He grinned mischievously. 'They never caught me.'

Annie found her voice. 'Where did you go?'

'Up tae the shieling. For a wee while I'd come doon the hill, tak milk fae one of the coos, eggs fae the hens. The minister gied me food, times, and a' summer there was berries and leaves to eat. At night I'd guddle for trout, or I'd snare a rabbit. But the winter came. It was that cauld. One day, men took the cows awa'. The fox got the hens. I wis starvin' o' hunger.'

Annie thought of the dead hens she'd found earlier.

Jock went on, 'I planted this yew tree on faither's grave. The minister was guid to me. He said ma mammy had got took awa' for *she* murdered Black Alastair.'

Annie put out a hand to touch his arm. It felt like cool air.

'I kept comin' back, hopin' mother would be home, so I could tell her. But I never found her. The minister said Black Alastair's family got put off his lands here, for displeasin' the queen. This auld hoose was built up again, for ither folk.' Angry tears spilled down his hollow cheeks. 'We shouldnae hae been cleared.'

Annie felt guilty, thinking how often she turned her mind away from the scene of the Clearance, because the memory frightened her so much.

Jock looked into Annie's eyes. 'I'm that weary o' waitin'.'

She said nothing till the thin shoulders stopped shaking. Then, as gently as she could, she said, 'Why me? Why did you decide to – haunt me? What can *I* do?'

'You're a lassie that has book-learnin'. I see'd you, through the windae, writin' and that. I *cannae* tak my freedom till I know whit happened tae Mother. I thocht maybe you might know …' His voice was softer than the air.

She whispered, 'I've read a *bit* about the MacKimbel men but – '

Such an expression of hope dawned in Jock's eyes.

A thought dawned in her head. 'Except – *some* of the MacKimbels must have got to Nova Scotia, because Jo-Ellen's descended from them.' Bits of the jigsaw were falling into place, though there were still big gaps. How could she complete the picture and see the whole story of what happened to Jock's mum?

'And it wisnae Mother who killed Black Alastair. No. I killed him, wi' my *sickle*. I wanted tae tell them it was me, but I was feart for my life. It was *my* fault she got took awa'.'

Annie remembered Jo-Ellen explaining how Jock might be haunting the museum because he'd committed a crime. The truth began fighting its way into her mind. But before it had time to break through, the sun popped blindingly up over the hill. Its beams silhouetted the blackened Gallows Tree, then flared out over the fields, picking out the white cottages. When she could see again, Jock had vanished.

Dad's voice called, 'Annie, where are you?' Then, after a moment's silence, 'Blinking blazes, who did this?'

He must have reached the hen-pen. Taking to her heels, Annie ran to meet him.

At breakfast, Dad explained how he must have been in such a state of shock after the thunderbolt last night that he'd forgotten to lock the hens in. 'I feel awful.'

'Well, it is awful, poor hens,' said Mum. 'But they left us their eggs.' She pulled one out from her apron pocket. 'If we keep them warm, they may hatch out in a few weeks. We could start again with new chickens.'

Dad looked up. 'We don't have an incubator.'

'True,' said Mum, 'But we can improvise.' She got out the ragged shirt. 'This'll be just the thing. We'll keep them in the airing cupboard. It's cosy in there.' She proceeded to wrap the eggs in the shirt, rolling the sleeves around them protectively.

Annie thought Jock would quite like this idea. Now she must try her best to find out about his mother.

After breakfast, Dad was just about to run Annie in to school when she realised Hot-Pot had vanished along with the rest of the little flock of sheep.

'They can't have got far,' she said. 'I'll go and find them.'

'You'll never get them back on your own,' said Dad.

Annie picked up the mobile phone. 'When I find them I'll ring you. Maybe old Tam would help?'

'Good idea,' said Mum. 'I'll ring the school and say you'll be in later.'

Annie took out her green bike and went tracking the sheep. You could tell from the line of droppings they'd left through the car park, which way they'd strayed. She found clues; bits of wool pulled off on thorn bushes and fences, nibbled grass, a sheepy smell on the air. The trail took her alongside the Clerks' fields towards the dark forestry plantation beyond, territory she'd never before explored.

Far up on the hill, Mr Clerk's rusty tractor was busy splattering slurry on another field, so she was quite safe.

Annie bumped and skidded her way along the side of the plantation. A brown animal leaped from the shadows and bounded away – a deer. Suddenly she heard 'Baaaahah'. Hot-Pot's bleat sounded exactly like a rough laugh. It came from somewhere deep among the trees. Dumping her bike at the side of the track, Annie plunged in among the sweet-smelling pines.

'Hot-Pot, you're a pain,' she called softly, pushing herself backwards through the prickly branches. The dark wood

closed in behind her, leaving no trace that anyone had ever been there.

Now a single sunbeam shimmered through a gap in the trees, lighting up a bright green mossy wall. Around the edges were yew trees, almost black, scattered with shrivelled blood-red berries that must once have looked so tempting, but which she knew were deadly poison.

The wall enclosed what might have been a sheep fank. Annie peered in.

It did indeed contain sheep. In a pool of golden sunlight, Hot-Pot and her pals meandered about calmly munching the lush new grass that grew among flat stone slabs. Not a sheep fank, but a graveyard! The one Sadie had seen? Only one stone stood upright.

A thought struck her. The sheep are walking over skeletons. Shivering, she could see the standing gravestone had lettering carved on it, covered with lichen. Maybe it would say 'MacKimbel'! She took a step nearer the entrance, beside which was a tumbledown building that might once have been a tiny chapel.

A low growl came from its doorway. Oh, there crouched a scruffy-looking collie! And a wee muddy puppy. How amazing – the dog was guarding the sheep, keeping them in the graveyard. And it wasn't going to let her past.

She fumbled for the mobile phone, to tell Dad the sheep were safe. Oh no, she'd left it tied in her bag on the back of her bike!

Engrossed, she bent to talk to the dog. And saw the dog looking beyond her. Who was there? Slowly she turned.

Across the track, his huge boots planted firmly in the mud, stood Murdo Clerk.

THE SICKLE

Murdo took a step towards Annie. 'I'd hae thocht a clever lassie the likes o' you could read notices,' he sneered. 'That yin there says "Private".' He pointed to a filthy felt-penned notice stuck to a tree.

Annie hadn't seen it. She backed away, frightened. She thought quickly; if I run, this big bully will catch me; if I argue, he'll just go mad.

To gain time, she said mildly, 'Our sheep got out. I came looking for them. This amazing dog has kept them safe. Whose is she?' Keeping her eyes on Murdo's face, she carefully stroked the dog.

Murdo's expression inexplicably softened. 'Bess here was my mother's dog.' The dog got up at the sound of her name, wagging her limp tail and nuzzling his hand.

'Your mother's? Er – tell me about her.' All the time Annie continued to back away from Murdo, further into the graveyard.

Murdo stroked the dog gently while he told Annie what a great shepherd his mum had been, how she'd been brilliant at training sheepdogs and how he'd had to hide Bess and her pup in the old chapel here to save them from his father. He ended, 'I cannae keep them here much longer. I'll have to find a better place. The pup'll be needin' fed proper, like.'

The sheep bunched in a corner, looking fearfully at Bess.

The gravestone was taller than Annie. She made sure it was between herself and Murdo. Oh, now she could read the writing. But it didn't say Mackimbel. 'Look,' she said, surprised. 'It says "Clerk".'

Murdo came closer. 'I never looked at it afore. Clerk, eh?' He sounded surprised too. And interested.

Hoping she'd diverted his thoughts from bullying, Annie started telling him all she'd learned about the local Clerk ancestry, rambling on about how some Clerks had emigrated to Canada.

Forgetting danger, she said, 'I was looking for a gravestone with "MacKimbel" on it. Did you ever see that name?'

He said, 'MacKimbel? No. Ma tellt me maist o' the grave-slabs frae here was nicked for buildin'. My granddad floored oor byre wi' them. It was supposed to be unlucky,' he grinned, 'but my granddad did okay. He was good wi' dogs and a'.' Murdo blushed and looked down. 'I'm supposed to be like him.'

He didn't seem quite so scary now. Maybe, because he wasn't having to show off in front of his pals?

Annie had an idea. 'S-Sadie has dogs. She might help – '

'Och yon Sadie's too full o' funny jokes,' Murdo spat.

Annie blethered on, 'Yes, but, if you're desperate – her Dad has kennels behind their house. He'd maybe take Bess and the puppy for a bit. Till you figure out what to do with them.' She swallowed. How on earth was she going to get out of this?

The puppy was climbing all over her feet, making little

yelps and wagging his tiny tail. He was really sweet. She bent to play with him.

From very far away came the sound of whistling, Duncan's tune. Bess loped away out of the enclosure, probably to investigate.

With a triumphant 'Baaahah', Hot-Pot cantered over the grass. She rammed her head at the back of Murdo's knees. The big boy simply buckled, folding quite gracefully down into the mud. Hot-Pot trotted off rolling her eyes.

Annie seized her chance. Leaping to her feet she sprinted out of the graveyard and into the trees.

* * *

Murdo picked himself up, cursing. The last of the sheep struggled past him, trotting away after the one that had butted him.

He shouldnae have trusted yon lassie. He might have known Annie'd be up to tricks, just like her pal Sadie Munro with her fish-gut jokes, and him supposed to be the hard man o' Glenmellish, leader of his village gang, the Rakers. But he'd get even. The gang was due to meet up, the nicht. They'd be plannin' their next mission. And he knew exactly who they'd be targetin' this time.

Far away he could hear Annie crashing through the trees. Would he go after her? No. Not now. He'd bide his time. Sadie Munro and Annie Campion might think they could get the better o' him, but they were wrang. Annie and her precious 'Museum Of Farming Life'. She should try the real farming life, life with his faither, where there was nothin' but work, work, work in the cauld and the rain and nae money for nothin'. Then she'd know a' aboot it. No, he had a better plan. He and the Rakers wid torch the Museum. And soon.

Breathless and frightened, Annie scrambled out from the last of the trees. She stopped to listen. Why was it so quiet? Could Murdo have taken a short cut and be lying in wait to pounce on her?

Silence.

Her green bike lay in the grass. She grabbed the phone. She switched it on.

Oh, now footsteps were coming through the wood!

With a 'Baahaaa', Hot-Pot erupted from the plantation, followed by the flock. The sheep stood around uncertainly, looking at Hot-Pot. Annie giggled with relief. From somewhere near, she heard a fainter giggle. Murdo wouldn't giggle. Was it Jock? Well, if it was, he needn't bother teasing her. He hadn't been much help when Murdo cornered her.

She spoke into the phone, 'I found the sheep,' and explained where they were.

Feeling a bit silly for being so scared, she cycled slowly homeward, surprised to find Hot-Pot trotting along behind her and the flock meekly following. Hot-Pot had clearly been promoted to head sheep.

At home, Mum and Dad were glaring at each other across the kitchen table. A torn letter lay there. They'd obviously been arguing.

Mum began slicing bread as if the loaf was someone she hated. She stabbed the knife into the cheese and hacked off hunks. What was up?

A vase of bluebells caught the sunlight from the window. Annie was glad to be safely home, and she was starving. She concentrated on eating while the storm raged over her head. Never had bread and cheese tasted so good.

'Right then,' said Mum. 'So what am I supposed to do?'

'What about?' asked Annie, pouring herself some milk.

Mum glared at her. 'That school I applied to for work – one of their art teachers suddenly announces she's going on sick leave. So they invite *me* to fill in for the rest of this term.'

Dad said, 'I'm saying we'll just have to manage without Mum, weekdays.'

Mum said, 'And *I'm* saying no way. If this *has* to be our last summer here I want to stay.' She got up. 'Oh, I don't know. I'll have to think about it. Come on Annie, I'll run you in to school.'

Annie gulped down her milk. 'Couldn't I just stay here?'

'You know the answer to that one, my girl. I rang Mrs McCrindle and told her I'd drop you off after lunch.'

'Okay.' Annie put her dishes in the sink.

Mum said, 'You'll go up to Sadie's after school?'

'Okay,' said Annie, brightening. 'Sadie's great-gran's going to be there. We want to talk to her.'

Mum said, 'Oh yes, for your Ancestors' project?' In the car, she said, 'You did well, bringing the sheep home.'

Annie told of her encounter with Murdo and how Hot-Pot had butted him.

Mum said thoughtfully, 'No wonder that Murdo's such a bully. They say his old man has been abominable to

98

everyone since his wife died. He certainly did his best to ruin our Gala Day with that revolting muck-spreader.'

At school, Duncan and Sadie were kneeling on the floor drawing faces for the Ancestor chart.

Sadie drew a scowly face with a down-turned mouth and dribbles coming out of it. Underneath she wrote, *Murdo Clerk*.

Duncan grinned, 'That's disgusting.'

'Tough,' said Sadie. 'I don't like yon big galoot.'

Mrs McCrindle got going on the afternoon's work. 'Local families were cleared from their homes so that sheep could become the main source of income for the landowners.'

'Where did the people go?' asked Annie, looking for corroboration of the stories she'd heard.

'Usually landowners chartered ships to take them away. Sometimes folk found ways to pay their own passages and like the boat-people of today, they didn't always end up where they'd expected to be. If they reached Canada, they'd be given a piece of land of their own. No longer would they have to pay a landlord or do what he told them. They'd be free. But many of the people drowned in the terrible Atlantic storms.'

Sadie flicked a paper pellet at Duncan. 'Aww,' she said.

'Thanks to Duncan, we now know that several families from Glenmellish did make it to Canada, where their descendants are now alive and well and doing very nicely indeed.'

Annie tried to imagine Jock's family sailing away from Ardmellish in a ship that looked like one of these galleons with dozens of sails billowing out like fat pillows. Had his mother drowned? Or had she reached Nova Scotia?

On the bus after school, Annie exaggerated her encounter with Murdo till she had Duncan and Sadie in fits of laughter.

This made her feel less scared of the memory.

They were still laughing as Duncan got off at his road end. Megabyte was waiting for him. It must be so great to have a dog to welcome you home after school.

Sadie's great-granny's ample figure almost filled the tiny kitchen, spreading chocolate nut paste thickly on slices of bread. 'Verra healthy,' she said, handing them one each. Her eyes twinkled cheerily. 'Yer ma's at work, Sadie. A young fella phoned. It's on the machine.'

Sadie looked surprised. 'A fella? Who?'

The old woman smiled. 'Somethin' aboot a dog. The Clerk boy – what's his name – oh, I cannae mind.'

Sadie squeaked, 'Murdo?'

'Murdo. Aye, that was it. He sounded right miserable that Coll wasnae in.' The old woman took a mug of tea and carried on talking as she went out to sit on the bench at the front door. Bracken the dog came and lay at her feet. 'You've no' tae phone him. He says he'll see you again.'

Annie's heart seemed to stop for a second. Was this a threat?

Sadie pressed the 'play' button on the answering machine. 'You have two messages,' it said. The first was from her mum; 'Sadie hen, make yoursel's a piece and jam, I'll be back soon.' The second had Sadie's eyes popping. Murdo's voice came through loud and clear and unusually posh; 'Eh, Coll, could you give us a bell? It's, eh, it's about my dogs.'

'My dogs?' Sadie mimicked Murdo. 'I'm phonin' him back.'

'No, leave it to Coll,' said Annie.

'Coll's no' here,' Sadie spoke through a mouthful of bread, chocolate spread widening her smile right up her cheeks.

Annie watched her dialling the number, wishing she wouldn't.

Sadie squinted her eyes, listening. 'They're a' oot,' she

whispered, as if Murdo could hear her. 'I'm gonnae leave a message.'

Annie heard the beep.

'This is Oban polis,' Sadie said in a deep voice. 'We are comin' tae arrest youse for stinkin' out Auchentibart wi' your muck-spreader. Beware, a alien.' She collapsed on the floor, laughing.

Annie protested, 'He'll think it's me.'

'He will no',' spluttered Sadie.

Annie had only seen Sadie's great-gran once before, on Gala Day, but she liked her. It wasn't long till they had her telling stories about days gone by in Ardmellish village.

Annie asked if she knew anything about the Clearances.

The old lady thought for a minute. 'I mind *ma* granny tellin' me about yon. Now wait a minute till I get it right in my head.' She paused.

Annie said, 'I was – told – Black Alastair cleared all the people from Auchentibart for his deer park.'

'But there was niver a deer park at Auchentibart, no.' The old lady warmed to her theme. 'Alastair's family did somethin' – I don't know what, but somehow they put the queen's nose out o' joint.'

'Queen Victoria?' asked Annie.

'Aye, likely. Anywy, the Queen wasn't pleased, and took away their lands. They say this Alastair would hurtle down the main street in his fancy carriage, his black horse at the gallop. And if a wean got in the way, too bad, he'd run it over. He'd hang a man for poachin' a rabbit. Everyone hated him. The people of the Glen named him Alasdair *Dubh* – Black Alastair. They say the folks at Auchentibart murdered him, in the end, and everyone was glad to be rid o' him.'

Sadie looked at Annie, her eyes wide open. 'Maybe it's the ghost of Black Alastair that's hauntin' you.'

'No,' said Annie, feeling as if her head was bursting. All these bits of stories. None of them quite tied in with each other, yet it seemed as if another tiny piece of the jigsaw had just slipped into place. 'I told you. The boy I've seen's called Jock MacKimbel. He's not much older than us.'

The old lady thought for a minute. 'MacKimbel. Well I never heard o' that name, hereabouts.' Her head slid to one side and she was asleep.

In the middle of *Neighbours*, the phone rang. Sadie jumped up. 'Jamil's takeaway,' she yelled, winking at Annie. Then, opening her eyes wide, 'Murdo Clerk, ye useless

muckle sumph!' A few minutes later, 'No way hosay.' Then she was silent, listening, scores of expressions flitting across her face, till Annie burst into laughter at her. Finally she screwed up her face as if sucking sour sweeties. 'We'll consider it, OK? Phone us back – me back – in hauf an hour, right?' She put the phone down with a clang, her eyes on Annie.

Annie said, 'What did he want?' half-knowing the answer.

'He wants us tae take in yon collie and her pup. That's a'. The cheek o' him!'

But Annie remembered the thinness of Bess, how wet and ill the old dog had looked. She'd told Sadie about her encounter with Murdo for a laugh. They all hated and feared Murdo, but the dog was different. 'Bess looked ill. She was shivering. She's just had a puppy, won't she need warmth and shelter and – and proper food?' Sadie knew lots about dogs.

Sadie twisted her skirt around. 'I'll need tae ask. There is an empty kennel round the back, but – '

Her great-granny woke up. Had she really been asleep? 'I'll mind Bess,' she said. 'Murdo Clerk's mither wis a guid lassie. I watched her train yon Bess.'

'But you cannae *hae* dogs in the home,' said Sadie.

'I'm here for my holidays, hen. I'll mind the auld dog, and Bracken here'll be company for her. Youse can decide what next when I'm gone.'

Annie said, 'Couldn't we make Murdo *do* something?'

'Just whit I wis thinkin', chookie hen,' said Sadie, screwing her face into a grimace.

Car wheels crunched on the track. Annie's Mum had arrived to take her home. She was a bit quiet in the car, as they drove away.

Annie thought she looked upset. Maybe she was still cross

and needed some distraction? She said, 'You know how I found the sheep in the wee graveyard?'

'Mmm.'

'Well, all the stones but one had fallen down or been stolen.'

'And?'

'Well, Jo-Ellen thought there might be one with MacKimbel on.'

'Who?' Mum wasn't really listening.

When they got home, a small lorry with chain saws piled in the back was reversing out of a parking space.

Mum said, 'Oh, they must have done the tree today.'

'The tree?' said Annie.

'Yes. The Gallows Tree. The one that nearly killed Dad in the thunderstorm. The lightning strike made it unsafe. The tree surgeon said he'd come and take a look and if necessary, chop it down.'

'Oh no,' wailed Annie, leaping out of the car. She slung her bag at the back door and ran down the path to see what had happened.

Clouds of smoke billowed into the air, smelling of hot pine resin from a pile of burning branches. Heaps of sawdust littered the ground. A neat pile of logs was stacked by the Auld Hoose doorway, their ends bright and raw looking. In front of its door lay a huge chunk of tree trunk, like a headless torso with cut-off limbs. But the lower half of the tree still stood, its branches flung wide. It had survived.

Annie examined the big piece of trunk. Some of the sap had oozed stickily from the cut edges. It smelt lovely.

But oh, what's this? A wooden handle. The handle of a sickle and – and its blade is embedded in the tree's flesh. It looks as if someone's been trying to chop the tree, got their sickle stuck, left it there and the poor tree has grown around it, covering it over with a huge scar.

Could the sickle even have been there since – since that night a hundred and fifty years ago when Jock MacKimbel had thrown it?

And now, as if a video replayed the scene in her head, everything came clear in Annie's mind. Jock *had* thrown his sickle at Black Alastair – and missed! She could see it now – the sickle flying through the air, skimming *past* the horse and whirling on towards the tree. The horse had reared up in fright. Black Alastair had fallen off, bashing his head against the tree. Neither Jock nor his mother had killed him, but the Gallows Tree itself. His death had been an accident. And Jock was innocent of any crime, though he didn't know it yet.

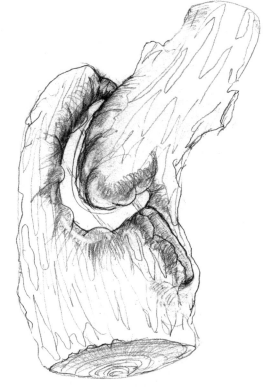

DOGS

Murdo tapped his foot. Where was the boys? For the first time, he noticed how the phone-box stank like the school lavvies. He did *not* want tae do this, and him the Rakers' top man, aye willin' to go one step further than the others. He wis strong enough tae blooter any o' them, or all together if necessary. Meeting up wi' the gang on a Friday night was the only laugh he ever got out o' life. So why would he be refusin' tae go out wi' them any more? If they knew it was because of a lassie, they'd laugh at him. And that he couldn't stand.

He flexed his shoulder muscles. The remains of the telephone dangled uselessly where he'd yanked it off its wall. Nobody'd tell Murdo Clerk what to do, least of all a wee scruff like Sadie.

He was still smarting from the telling-off she'd given him. 'If ye want us tae take in your dogs, stop yon gang o' eejits pesterin' everyone in Glenmellish. Or your dogs is oot. Geddit?'

How meekly he'd promised. He'd made his voice sound whiny, so she'd feel sorry for him. He'd do anything for the sake of Bess.

'Right then.' Now Sadie sounded like his Ma used to, sort of comforting, as though she was talking to a wee boy. 'Me and the old lady'll tak' Bess and the pup for a wee while, but if we hear youse have been getting' up to any more o' your nonsense, they're out the door. Right?'

He wished he'd got Coll on the phone instead of wee Sadie. You could talk tae a fella, but lasses? Gie him a break. Anyway, he could relax now. For a while, Bess and the pup were safe, well away from his father and out of the rain. So, for the time being, he'd make the gang lie low. The Rakers did what he told them.

One of the lads was coming down the road. It'd be Sandy. He was always the first. The others would be late as usual. They were to plan their next attack; Murdo had suggested the Museum. Had he the power to stop them, now? They'd only just begun to get the hang of fire raising, making the wee pile of fags that burned nice and slow so they could all get out the way, watch the blaze from somewhere else. The police blamed passing tourists for flinging fags out their motors. What a laugh.

Murdo pulled the black balaclava down over his face. When he and the lads went out, they went anonymous.

* * *

On Saturday morning, Annie was helping Dad in the Visitor Centre when the post van came with the mail.

'Sort that lot out, will you, Annie?' asked Dad. 'Looks like there's still nothing from the Tourist Board.'

She enjoyed this job, making three piles, one each for the

Museum, Mum and Dad. 'What about the Hassan Trust?' she asked.

'Blinking blazes,' said Dad. 'What's the date today? The deadline must be quite soon and we haven't had a minute to discuss what we're going to do.'

'I've had an idea,' said Annie.

'Okay, let's talk about it later. This one's for Mum. It's from that school.'

'Oh no.'

'Better take it to her. She's teaching a weaving group down in the Auld Hoose.'

Annie followed the burn along to the wee bridge. She *could* just drop the letter into the water and let it float away. But Mum and Dad were great parents and she loved them. She wished they didn't have all these money worries. For the only thing that really *mattered* was that they were a happy family. From now on she'd stop girning about going back to the town. But, oh, how she wished they could stay here at Auchentibart for ever and ever.

The water gurgled beneath her feet. Who would help Jock if she wasn't here?

A small group of people was leaving the Auld Hoose. The workshop must be over.

Inside, Mum sat at the loom.

'Letter for you.' Annie reluctantly handed it over.

'Thanks, love.' Mum unpeeled the envelope, pulled out the letter and read it. Then she pushed it into her pocket, along with her scissors, shuttle and a bundle of wool. Together they set off up the path.

Annie said, 'Couldn't we *both* persuade Dad we should stay a bit longer?'

Mum sighed. 'You're right, Annie. How can I leave now, just when the summer tourist season is beginning? I'm not going to take this teaching job. Maybe next year, if I have to.'

Annie said encouragingly, 'We have been busier, haven't we?' A wave of hopefulness spread through her.

Mum hugged her. 'True. What we need now is a great idea so we can try for the Hassan Trust. That money would make all the difference – Jo-Ellen says they're really generous, if they believe in what you're trying to do. It's just so hard to find the time for thinking something up ...'

'You don't have to,' said Annie, 'I've *got* a great idea.' Putting plates on the kitchen table for lunch, she said, 'Why don't we make ourselves into a Clan Centre?'

'A what?' Mum stirred soup.

'A Clan Centre. The teacher told us how some clans have their own centres in Scotland. Descendants come to find out about their families. They have clan gatherings and stuff. We could start one here.'

'Mmm,' said Mum. Not a bad idea. But what clan? Surely they've all got a place, if they want one?'

'The MacKimbels haven't.'

'The who?'

'MacKimbels. They were once the weavers here. And Jo-Ellen's ancestors were MacKimbels from somewhere in Glenmellish, till they got cleared. Duncan's found out about lots of them, by the Internet. Well this could be *their* Clan Centre – a meeting place for MacKimbels from all over the world.'

'Ye-es,' Mum sounded doubtful.

Annie was getting more enthusiastic the more she thought about it. 'Maybe they've got a tartan? We could have a website, we could – '

Dad came in, 'We could have lunch, by the smell of things. Mmm, I'm starving. What's all the excitement, about young lady?'

Mum ladled out soup, which smelled delicious. 'Our Annie has come up with an idea. And I think she might have hit on something really good.'

* * *

On Sunday morning Sadie rang. 'Annie,' her voice sounded conspiratorial, 'can ye come doon here?'

'Why?'

'Big Murdo's bringin' his dogs. Come doon for the laugh. He's due here in an hour.'

Annie got out her green bike. As she cycled up the hill towards Sadie's, she remembered falling off, and the little dell where Jock had bound up her knee. She'd checked the Ordnance Survey and discovered the spring there was called Mairi's Well. It was the source of the burn that ran through the Museum fields.

Minutes after she got to Sadie's, Murdo roared up on a quad bike, Bess and the pup wobbling about in a box on the back. She watched through the kitchen window as the old dog Bracken ran out into the road, barking and growling at Bess.

Sadie whispered to Annie, 'Wait here. And keep quiet.' She went to the door.

Annie could hear their voices as Murdo's heavy boots clumped in to the kitchen.

He was saying, 'Eh, is Coll in?'

Sadie yelled, 'Coll! It's yon bampot, Murdo.'

Annie cringed. Murdo would belt Sadie one.

But Murdo was saying, 'It's, eh, very guid o' ye, Sadie lass.' Annie could hear his boots shuffling on the flagstone floor.

Sadie said, 'And mind the bargain. Did ye tell yon thugs to stop their vandalisin' nonsense?'

Murdo coughed and cleared his throat. 'Aye, aye. I did.'

Annie heared thumps as Coll bounded down the stair. 'Hey, Murdo,' he said. 'I hear you've got banned fae the gang,' he laughed.

Murdo grunted.

Coll said, 'Come away and we'll get your dogs into the kennel.'

Annie heard their footsteps going away.

Sadie stuck her head round the door. 'Bide there a minute, till Murdo's away.' A few minutes later she hissed, 'Oh wheesht, they're comin' back.'

Murdo was saying, 'Aye weel, I'm for it noo. The Rakers weren't best pleased when I tellt them no' tae go out any more. Sandy '

'The polisman's boy?' came Coll's voice.

'Aye, him.' Murdo sniffed loudly. 'He says, "You'd better watch your back, big Murdo. The Rakers goes on, eh, fellas?" And the rest o' them were wi' *him*, no wi' me.' He sounded mystified. 'I never done them no harm, nor nothin'. "Watch yer back, sonny boy", is a' the thanks I get.'

Coll said, 'I thought gangs was supposed to stay loyal and that.'

Murdo snorted, 'Aye, right. I says, "We'll just suspend operations for a wee while," I says. "Who're you to tell us what to do?" says yon Sandy.'

Coll said, 'Are you feart o' them?'

Murdo coughed again. 'No' me. I'm no' feart o' nothin', man.'

Coll said, 'Is that your Dad's quad out there?'

Their footsteps receded as Murdo laughed a bit too loudly for conviction, 'Aye, and he doesnae know I've got it. I'd better be getting' back. Cheers – oh, and thanks for takin' in Bess. I'll, eh, sort somethin' out soon for her.'

When Murdo scuttered away on the quad, Coll went out with Bracken. Sadie took Annie round to the kennels behind the house.

The kennels turned out to be three wooden huts painted green, with sloping roofs and little doors. In front of each was a concrete-floored pen surrounded with high green railings. In one, Bess stood, whining a little, her head on one side, as if she was asking questions like, where's Murdo gone? Why am I here?

'It's a'right, lass,' said Sadie, going in and offering a bread crust. 'You're tae bide wi' us a wee while.'

Bess took the bread delicately and let Sadie pat her. Annie followed, and stroked her nose. Bess wagged her limp tail a little.

'She hasnae got much energy,' said Sadie, 'and she's as thin as a rake.' She felt along the dog's side, where the ribs stood out. 'We'll feed ye well, lass.'

The puppy came skittering across the concrete and made straight for Annie. 'Oh, he's so nice,' she said, picking him up and stroking the wriggling body.

Sadie looked up. 'He's nae use,' she said. 'He's deaf.'

'How d'you know?' To Annie he looked perfect, mostly white, with a little black saddle mark on his back, and his black tail with a white bit on the end.

'Murdo tell't me. He'll no can mind the sheep, he'll be nae use on the farm. He should hae been put down at birth, but Murdo couldnae do it.'

'Murdo –? But he's so tough.'

'He is no'. He's a big softie. He just acts tough, to impress his mates, and keep his faither aff his case. I keep tellin' him tae staun' up to his old man. I can mak' him do onythin', just watch me,' Sadie grinned.

Annie remembered how it hadn't been so very difficult

to talk to Murdo that day at the graveyard. Maybe she shouldn't have been so scared of him after all.

The puppy began to chew her sleeve. She said, 'Won't he get better?'

'Who, Murdo?' Sadie googled her eyes at Annie.

'The puppy,' Annie giggled.

'Daddy says a lot o' collies that's born wi' white heads or white ears turns out tae be stone deaf. And there's no cure.'

'So, what'll happen to him?' asked Annie. The puppy felt warm and cuddly in her arms.

Sadie came over to stroke him. 'It's a blue do, right enough,' she said, unusually thoughtful. 'But och, we'll think o' somethin', won't we son?'

'Has he got a name yet?' Annie reluctantly put the puppy down, but he wouldn't leave her. He sat on her shoe, looking up at her.

Sadie said, 'That's it. We'll ca' him Blue. Ma favourite colour. Okay?'

'Okay,' said Annie.

Meanwhile, heading for the windswept farm, Murdo was driving into trouble.

An old crow perched on a chimney high above the farmhouse roof. It usually hung about there, waiting for unwary creatures to be squashed on the road and provide it with dinner – maybe a juicy weasel or a young rabbit. It's eye brightened as the quad bike roared up the track. It saw farmer Clerk come out, climb aboard his tractor and speed out of the yard. And it flew up squawking in fright when tractor and quad crashed into each other at the corner.

How it all happened no-one could later quite explain; perhaps old Clerk swerved too suddenly, perhaps the track ruts were too deep. But next thing, the tractor was on its side and the old farmer was yelling his head off, pinned beneath the wreckage. Murdo, tipped off the quad, stood rubbing his elbow, shaking his head and gawping at his purple-faced father while the crow flew away to the woods in disgust.

The crash was heard down at the Museum.

'What was that?' Dad asked Mum.

'Look,' she pointed out of the window. 'They must be burning old tyres up at Clerk's farm.' She lifted the ragged shirt out of the airing cupboard. 'No signs of life in these eggs yet. Maybe it's early days.'

Dad wrinkled his nose. 'I wish to goodness Annie would get rid of that thing. It keeps appearing, like it's got a life of its own.'

FIRE!

When Annie came home, Mum and Dad were struggling to fill in the last part of the Hassan Trust form.

'This Clan Centre idea,' said Dad. 'What exactly are we going to call it?'

Annie thought for a minute, 'MacKimbel Weavers? Like, we *are* weaving. Well, Mum is.'

'Sounds like a factory,' complained Dad. 'And we're not MacKimbels.'

Mum looked up. 'The Macdonalds call their place the Clan Donald Centre.'

Dad shook his head. 'Too plain.'

'Oh Dad,' said Annie, more than a touch of impatience in her voice.

'Keep calm,' said Mum.

Annie struck a pose. 'I've got it. "Auchentibart Museum, Ancestral Home of Clan MacKimbel." And underneath, "Argyllshire Weavers", right?'

Mum and Dad looked at each other and nodded.

Dad said, 'We'd have to repaint the sign.'

'Oh Dad,' chorused Annie and Mum.

And so it was agreed. Dad filled in the last bit of the form, signed it at the bottom and stuffed it into a new envelope.

Out on the main road beyond the Museum an ambulance siren wailed.

'That's travelling fast,' Mum observed. 'Must be an accident somewhere.'

'Won't it be brilliant if we get the money?' Annie got up from the table.

Dad sniffed. 'If.'

'If we get it,' Mum said dreamily, 'we might have enough money to install a bigger loom. I could – '

Dad got up. 'There'll be plenty of time for dreaming *if* the Trust accepts us. They won't be short of applicants.'

Mum said, 'Annie's idea might turn out to be what saved us.' She gave Annie a hug.

'Yes, well done. All we need now is a good rating from the blinking Tourist Board,' said Dad.

As Annie was getting ready for bed, the ambulance siren sounded again, the note of its horn making a downward wail as it passed along the road.

Mum said anxiously, 'I wonder who's in trouble? Hope it's no one we know.'

Dad said, 'Reckless drivers, no doubt. Too many on that road. Goodnight, Annie.'

'Sleep well, love,' said Mum. 'And dream about what you'd like for your birthday next week.'

* * *

Annie came home from school with the information, next day. 'It was the Clerks. Murdo got hurt. Sadie was upset.'

Mum said, 'Yes, her mother told me. That stupid boy, Murdo, went out on the farm quad bike. Of course, he's under age. It seems he and his dreadful father were arguing about a dog or something. Murdo stamps off, grabs the quad and roars off down the track in a rage. Eventually, old Clerk gets worried.'

'That's a first,' said Dad.

'True,' said Mum. 'Anyway, he's driving out of the yard on his way to look for Murdo when the boy, who's on his way home, careers round the corner and – bang!'

'Blinking blazes,' said Dad.

'So, will they be okay?' said Annie, inexplicably worried about Murdo.

'Murdo got off lightly, just a bit of bruising. But old Clerk – at the last minute he turned the tractor, too fast. It fell over, landed on him. His leg's crushed to pulp. The hospital don't know if they can save it.'

Dad said, 'Poor sod. Lucky he wasn't crushed to death, old rascal.'

* * *

On Annie's birthday, both cards from her grandparents had a dog on them, one a Dalmatian, the other a curly poodle. There was a package with Canadian maple leaf stamps all over it. The plan was for Sadie and Duncan to come up for tea after the Museum's closing time.

'We'll keep, er, presents till the evening,' said Dad. 'Okay, Annie?'

The excitement was almost unbearable.

At six o'clock Sadie, Duncan and Megabyte arrived. Soon they were seated round the table singing 'Happy birthday' to Annie, with Megabyte howling along.

The birthday cake was made of chocolate. It was shaped like a sort of Scottie dog, with a tartan collar. Annie wished as hard as she could, blowing out the candles. Now for the presents.

She opened the Canadian one first. Jo-Ellen had sent a card with a husky dog on it and an empty book with a green cover. Gold lettering said, 'Annie Campion's Journal'. There was also a video with a handwritten label: *Locations for Heartland 1*. It didn't look much good – no pictures to show what it was about. She put it aside.

Next, Duncan's parcel; used yellow computer print-out paper decorated with felt-pen squiggles. Inside was a CD of their favourite folk group.

Duncan grinned, 'It's got yon tune on it. You know?'

'Jock's tune? Oh, amazing. Thanks,' she said.

Sadie's present was wrapped in red and green Christmas paper with bits of old sellotape hanging off it. Inside was a blue plastic dog's bowl with DOG in white letters. 'It's for – when ye need it,' Sadie smirked mischievously at her.

'Thanks,' said Annie. She'd add it to her collection of doggie things.

Dad had disappeared. Mum was smiling all over her face.

He came back with a plain cardboard box. Something inside it was wobbling about. Megabyte barked as Dad laid it on the ground. 'Go on, open it,' he laughed.

Annie undid the top. Oh! Unbelievable! Blue, the puppy, gazed up at her, wagging his tail and whimpering. She scooped him up in her arms, so happy she could hardly speak. 'Thank you,' she whispered, nuzzling his head. All sorts of feelings whirled through her at once: Is he really mine? Will I be able to look after him properly? Will he *like* belonging to me? She buried her face in his soft warm fur.

Megabyte came to sniff him and seemed to approve. Everyone crowded round to look.

Eventually Annie's face emerged. 'What about Murdo?'

Sadie blushed. 'Me and Murdo agreed it. And your Dad paid him, okay.'

'Me and Murdo?' said Annie, temporarily distracted. 'So, you've made up with him?'

'Aye.' Sadie giggled. 'So long as he behaves hisself. Murdo's awright. He's off the school, lookin' after the sheep and that till his Dad's out the hospital. Coll's tae help him, weekends. Murdo's that pleased.'

Mum said, 'And is he behaving himself better in the village?'

Sadie made a face. 'The Rakers, ye mean? He wouldnae dare go back out wi' them. Not if he wants me tae speak to him.'

* * *

The wind blew harder all weekend, and by Bank Holiday Monday it brought rain. Duncan came up to keep Annie company while she was minding the Auld Hoose. They sat on the doorstep while Megabyte frisked around outside, playing with Blue and chasing rabbit smells.

'That dog's mad,' said Duncan. 'Look at her.' He smiled indulgently.

'So's mine,' said Annie. 'Specially at night. He keeps waking me up.'

'He'll be missing his mum still.' Duncan looked sad for a minute. 'But he'll get used to being on his own. He'll be more settled in a week or two. So, it's outside every hour and four feeds a day?'

'Mmhm. Duncan, was it easy, training Meg?'

'Terrible,' Duncan grinned. 'She's got a mind of her own. You start right away working with Blue, now. Make it a game, teaching him to sit when you tell him.' He looked away up the burn to where it disappeared into the trees. 'Annie?'

'Yes?'

'Have you seen Jock?'

Annie felt guilty again. 'No.'

'So, you haven't told him all we found out? And about the sickle being in the tree?'

'No.'

'What have you done with it?'

Duncan followed her into the Auld Hoose. She took the sickle down from a rusty hook. 'I've been going to give Jock's shirt back too, but I keep forgetting, okay?' Her voice came out crosser than she meant it to.

A gust of wind rattled the dry thatch above their heads. Suddenly the atmosphere changed. The clouds outside thickened, making it darker and darker.

Annie pulled the door to. Carefully she struck a match and lit one of the storm lanterns. The smell of hot paraffin wafted about. Windy draughts moaned through the rafters like souls in torment.

Duncan wandered around the dark interior of the Auld Hoose, looking at the bits of furniture and picking up pots and kettles. He began to whistle.

Suddenly the door burst open. Jock stood there, almost transparent, his hair whipping about his thin face. His eyes were staring, terrified.

'Jock! What is it, man?' said Duncan.

Annie stood stock still, catching Jock's fear. 'What's wrong? Oh, Jock, we've – I've been meaning to tell you – I'm sorry – '

But a burst of air snatched the flimsy ghost away, his mouth stretched wide open as if he was screaming something, but the only sound Annie could hear was the howling of the wind.

The storm lantern went out. Something heavy fell outside. The door crashed shut.

* * *

Murdo stepped off the bus at Sadie's road-end. He shouldered the heavy bag of dog food and pulled up the hood of his parka. What a night, wind and rain like it was winter.

He thought over what his father had said in the hospital. 'I want ye in wi' me, son, workin' the farm. I wouldnae be here today if you hadnae got me out frae under yon tractor. No' bad, son. You're a strong lad. Maybe I've no' been a' that I should have been, since your Ma went and maybe I'm sorry. It'll be different now.' More words than Faither had ever said to him in one go.

It wouldn't be an easy life, the hill farm. But it was what

he wanted, what he was bred to. He'd just said, 'A'right, Faither,' and given a wee smile. Now he squared his shoulders. Maybe together, workin' instead o' fightin', they'd mak a go of it. He was feelin' good. Like, more o' a man, these days.

'Is, eh, wee Sadie in?' he asked Coll, standing at the door, after a bit of chat.

Coll grinned at him, 'You'd better no' ca' her wee, this weather. Come in.'

Tugging at his dripping hair to get it into some sort of order, Murdo shambled in after him.

Sadie was lookin' awful pretty, sittin' on the hearthrug between Bracken and Bess. When she looked at you wi' thon big blue eyes, you'd do anything she asked you.

Murdo cleared his throat. 'Haw, hen, I picked up a bag o' dog food for youse. Bess must hae been feedin' well, her coat's that glossy.'

Sadie fluttered her eyelashes at him. 'I'm good wi' dogs. And ither animals.'

Bess whacked her tail on the rug. She got up stiffly to greet him.

Murdo patted her roughly. 'I've came to tak you home wi' me, lass. You'll no' need tae work no more. You'll be, eh, retired.'

Sadie said, 'You'll no tak' her in yon rain.'

After a bit of an argument, she got her way. He'd leave Bess till the next day.

It was late when Murdo set off on the long walk up the hill to his farm. Twilight was deepening fast. The westerly gale whipped his hair into his eyes. Out of habit, he scanned what he could see of the countryside, looking for sheep. This weather wasnae good for the wee lambs, out on the hill. They could cope wi' cold, but no' the wet. And you aye needed tae watch what was goin' on; a fox wid take a weak lamb no bother.

He lumbered up the rise above the main road. Not far to go now. From here he overlooked Auchentibart Museum. A couple of lights glimmered from the Campions' windows.

Suddenly his eyes caught movement. Five dark shapes clambered over the fence from the Museum field and up to the main road. They were shoving each other about, rolling on the ground. Through the shrieking of the wind, he could hear their laughter.

The Rakers.

Shrugging his shoulders, Murdo turned away. Whatever they were up to, he wanted no part in it. Sadie was worth goin' straight for, and he had more interesting things to do than messin' about with thon gang o' wee boys.

As he came over the brow of the hill, the wind stopped. It must be going to change direction. In the silence, he turned to take a last look down the glen before moorland hid his view.

A small red light appeared, down the glen below the Museum. The tail light o' a motorbike? But why wasn't it moving?

Fascinated, Murdo watched. The light expanded. Now it was turning golden … He thought of UFOs. 'Take me to your leader' you'd say to an alien. And you'd be whapped away in a flying saucer. Load o' nonsense.

He felt the new wind on his face. Sure enough it was coming up the glen from the east now, smelling faintly of smoke; not the reek of peat, coal or logs, but a musty dampness like when old rags begin smouldering on your midden.

There came a crackling sound. Like a firework, the golden glow exploded into tongues of orange flame. The Rakers must have set somebody's old hay bales alight. Waste o' time.

Suddenly it was as if a whole set of keys turned together, unlocking his brain. The Rakers had gone on with the plan, to torch the Museum.

Vaguely he thought of Sadie's friend. If anything happened to Annie, he'd be in trouble. His mind turned slowly.

He should call the fire station. Yes, but he'd wrecked the only public phone box for miles. No point going back down there then. Better get home, phone from there. Yes, but what fireman would believe him after all the spoof calls he'd made, and he a known hellraiser? Okay, then get back to the farm and phone the Museum folks. Warn them. They might no' have noticed the fire yet.

Stumbling uphill over the lumpy heather, he broke into a run.

* * *

The Museum kitchen was full of steam. Moira was dyeing wool, dance music full blast on the radio.

Keith put down the phone. 'Where on earth can Annie have got to?' He looked anxiously at Moira. 'Sadie hasn't seen her all day.'

'Have you tried Duncan?' she said.

'Yes, but their phone's out of order.'

Moira stirred vigorously. 'She'll be fine. She's sensible. And I know she's taken the pup. She'll be showing him off to Duncan's gran.'

Keith pulled on his boots. 'I'm going over there. She's never been out this late without us knowing where she is.'

'Okay, love, but think about it. Annie and Duncan usually walk the old drover's track. The car won't cope with it so – '

But Keith had left, dragging his anorak over his head. She heard the car engine rev, then roar away into the wind. Somewhere far away, a dog barked frantically.

* * *

Murdo gasped for breath, running now towards his farm track. As he reached the gateway the first stone hit his leg. Another hit him on the shoulder. Sticks and twigs began raining down on him till he stopped, bewildered, his arms over his face.

'Sandy, stop it,' he yelled. Somehow the Rakers must have overtaken him, though how –?'

A bony hand dug into his arm, pulling at him. In the darkness he could see it was a raggedy boy. There was a niff off him, of cows, peat. It wasn't Sandy, who usually smelt of aftershave these days.

'Get aff me,' Murdo shouted. 'What is it ye want?'

The boy was dragging him back the way he'd come, hitting him over the head and shoulders with a whippy branch. Soon he was chasing him as if Murdo was a sheep, herding him all the way back down the brae towards the Museum.

Smoke and flame belched upward from one of the cottages. The thatch was well alight, casting a fearsome scarlet glow over everything. The heat grew more intense the nearer Murdo got.

With a last shove, the boy pushed Murdo at the burning building.

A bicycle caught his eye. It had fallen across the entrance, jammed against the door by a huge lump of tree trunk. It

was green. Jeez, it was Annie Campion's bike. Could she be inside? No way could anyone open the door with the bike stuck like that.

Shreds of burning thatch began to blow around in the wind. The roof would collapse any minute now.

Using all his weight, Murdo heaved at the tree trunk. It wouldn't move. A piece of burning thatch fell and singed his arm. He yelped with pain and kicked out. The trunk shifted a little. He kept going. When it rolled, he went his length, leapt to his feet and threw the bike away. Before he had time to yank the door it burst outward in flames.

* * *

In the kitchen, Moira looked up. The car was back almost as soon as it had left. Keith must have found Annie. She heard running footsteps.

But Keith was yelling, 'The Auld Hoose is burning.' He rushed in and grabbed the phone. '999 – we're on fire. Where? Auchentibart Museum. Get the boys out here as fast as you can. The other cottages could go up too, in this wind. Okay, okay, here's the address. No, nobody lives in it … I don't believe this. The fire engine's been called out on another assignment, you think it's a spoof, but it's a house with people in it so it has priority?'

A dog – Duncan's Megabyte – had come in with him. She was barking hysterically round his feet. Behind her trailed the puppy, Blue, soaking wet.

Moira shrieked, 'Annie? Where's Annie?' She ran out crying, 'Annie was minding the Auld Hoose. She'd never leave the puppy. Something dreadful must have happened.'

THE RAINBOW

Burning thatch sparked angrily above Annie's head. She couldn't see. Hot smoke stung her eyes. Fumes choked her chest and she couldn't breathe properly.

Terrified, she pushed and shoved at the door. Why wouldn't it open?

Suddenly the old wood cracked and gave way. Annie felt cool air rush past her. She fell through onto the ground, gasping for breath, passing out.

She was being picked up. Carried along at a run. Dumped in cold water.

The shock brought her round. She tried to yell, 'Get Duncan,' but it came out as a coughing fit. She rubbed at her sore eyes. Her lungs felt full of grit.

Although she was sitting in the burn, trying to breathe, splashing water into her face to clear her vision, she could feel the heat.

The Auld Hoose blazed like a furnace. The windows were like fiery eyes, the door like a gaping mouth spitting flame. Showers of scarlet sparks swirled up and away in the wind.

Shivering, Annie crawled out of the water.

A black figure ran towards her and threw what looked like a bundle of rags into the water beside her.

Hissss!

As the flames were extinguished, Annie croaked, 'Duncan!'

'Is onybody else in there?' came a man's voice.

'No,' wheezed Annie.

Duncan was being dragged out onto the bank. Steam rose from his clothes. He lay very still.

Annie's whole body shuddered uncontrollably. As she crawled towards her friend, a terrifying roar came from the Auld Hoose. Flames leapt skyward. With a crash, the roof fell in.

* * *

By the time the first fire appliance arrived, Annie was fast asleep. The doctor had come to check them out, sending Duncan to hospital 'just to be on the safe side'.

When Annie woke, her chest and throat still hurt from the smoke. She picked up the puppy. There was no one in the kitchen. The back door hung open. The rain had stopped but the morning air was thick with the reek of charred wood. So, it hadn't all been a bad dream.

Mum came trailing along the track, her head down.

Annie ran to meet her, saying, 'The Auld Hoose – ?'

Mum was crying. 'Only the walls are left.' She threw her arms round Annie. 'Oh love, what a terrible night. Thank goodness *you're* all right. That's the only thing that really matters.'

Blue wriggled out of Annie's grasp and landed on the ground. She said, 'Is Duncan okay?'

'His gran phoned. The hospital says he'll probably get home tomorrow. Luckily he only has superficial burns from where his anorak sleeves caught fire. His arms will be sore for a bit, but he'll be fine. She said the crazy boy was trying

to save some old sickle? And he wanted you to know he managed to throw it out safely. Does this make any sense to you?'

'Yes,' said Annie. 'Yes it does. I'll tell you – oh, some other time, Mum.' She thought, how awful, if Duncan had died in the fire, because of her. It was bad enough that he'd been hurt. For Duncan was her friend. He was real. He mattered more than any ghost.

Dad came up the path, his eyes red-rimmed, his face blackened, talking to himself. 'That's it then. Where am I supposed to find the money to repair the Auld Hoose? Insurance? Ha, don't make me laugh.'

Mum interrupted, 'Keith, does anyone know who saved our kids?'

'No idea.'

'We must find out. Whoever it was deserves a bravery award.' She hugged Annie again.

Another thought struck Annie: if Jock's appearance had truly been to warn her of some terrible danger, then this *must* have been the disaster he'd been foretelling. So it was over.

Hot-Pot trotted towards them, her white skin dotted with flakes of black fall-out from the fire. 'Bahaa,' she bleated. 'Baahaa.'

Annie began to giggle. 'Hot-Pot, you look like a Dalmatian.'

Blue crouched at the path side, then bounced up and woofed at the sheep.

Hot-Pot lowered her head, took a run – and butted him.

Blue hurtled away yelping, his tail between his legs.

Annie ran after him, picked him up and stuffed him inside her jacket. Looking scared, he kept his eyes fixed on Hot-Pot.

Suddenly Annie, Mum and Dad began to giggle. Soon they were helpless with mirth. Later, laughing and clutching their sides, arms around each other, they managed to stagger in to the kitchen.

* * *

At school, the Ancestor Chart looked great up on the wall, completed at last. The green tissue-paper tree had loads of names on it

'Well done, children,' the teacher had said. 'A very good piece of work.'

Annie read from Duncan's pile of e-mails; *Hi, Duncan, my ancestors were McCaimbels of Auchentibart, Glen-mellish, transported here after the Clearances. Your friends' idea of starting a Clan Centre there is great and I'd be happy to send them a small donation. Give me their address? Yours with best wishes, Morgan McCaimbel, Albany, Australia.* 'Sounds nearly the same as MacKimbel, different spelling. Maybe it's Australian? Any more, Duncan?'

'Three.' Duncan picked up the print-outs; 'All legit MacKimbels. One from New Zealand, the others from Nova Scotia. And they're all offering help.'

Later, Annie said, 'Duncan?'

'Mhmm?'

'The Auld Hoose fire. Would you call that a disaster?'

Duncan gave her a look. 'We nearly got fried. And the place was burned down. I'd call that a disaster. Hey, wasn't it amazing the way Megabyte took your puppy home?'

Annie nodded. 'Meg's great. So, would that fire be what Jock was – warning me about?'

'Could be.'

Annie said, 'I keep thinking he's around, but he never

quite appears. Then I think – maybe I'm just imagining him sort of, like remembering him?'

Duncan said, 'Maybe you don't see him properly because you don't deserve to. You have to tell him the truth – and give him back his shirt.'

'Right,' said Annie, feeling guilty. 'Soon.'

Duncan said, 'What's the idea of the barbie at your place tonight?'

'We're celebrating staying on.'

After closing time at the Museum Annie sat on the field gate, her bare toes rubbing Hot-Pot's back. Blue played around, woofing at the sheep, who looked down her nose at him, not scared at all. The sun shone, birds sang and the breeze drifted in from the south-west smelling of thyme and flowers. How could anyone bear to leave this place?

All their friends and acquaintances from Ardmellish village and the surrounding glen piled into the Visitor Centre that evening. Sadie and Coll even brought Murdo with them. The men all helped each other toss skewers of meat, corn on the cob, sausages and potatoes onto the barbecue while the children handed round tartan paper plates and napkins and red plastic cutlery. Soon everyone was eating and drinking and talking all at once, helping themselves to crisps and ice-cream and pies and jellies till they were practically bursting.

After a while, the sky clouded over and a few spots of rain began to fall.

In the Visitor Centre, Dad made a speech. 'Welcome to Auchentibart Museum. Moira, Annie and I would like to thank you all for your continuing support and for coming to join in our celebration tonight.

'We have three announcements to make: One, I've just heard that we're to feature in the Tourist Board's book next year, *and* we're to be highly commended. Two, I had an unofficial phone call from Ardmellish House this afternoon, to say the Hassan Trust likes our idea of becoming the MacKimbel Clan Centre and they're going to give us generous financial support for the next *three years*, so we can plan ahead. And three? Ah. We'll keep three till after you've had a chance to view the little film Jo-Ellen sent Annie for her birthday. We thought you'd like to share it. Enjoy.' And with a flourish, he switched on the TV.

Heartland Locations 1 was the title. The screen flickered for a moment, then Jo-Ellen's voice said, 'Why Auchentibart Museum, Glenmellish, is the ideal location for our film.'

As Annie watched, familiar scenes came to life. At first, she felt sleepy as Jo-Ellen's voice droned on about how Black Alastair had caused misery in the glen.

But she woke up when Jo-Ellen said Chrissie MacKimbel had tried to change him.

Black Alastair had fallen in love with pretty Chrissie MacKimbel, but his father forbade their marriage, insisting the fermtoun be cleared, bribing Alastair with promises of a deer park in the hope of persuading him to forget Chrissie.

The letter C embroidered on Jo-Ellen's scrap of fabric must have stood for Chrissie!

Annie was really surprised at the next bit. It told how the old minister had arranged a secret wedding for Black Alastair and Chrissie. *Unknown to the old Laird, they were made man and wife. A year later, Black Alastair could no longer stand up to his father. He bought passages to Canada for himself and his young wife and attempted to warn her before he was sent to clear her family. But that terrible night at Auchentibart, the MacKimbels murdered him.*

'Oh no they didn't,' Annie hissed into Duncan's ear.

The remains of the MacKimbel family were rounded up

and sent by sea to Nova Scotia.

'Except for Jock MacKimbel,' Annie said.

Now the video was showing scenes from Gala Day. There was old Tam shearing Hot-Pot's fleece off, Sadie spinning wool, and Duncan playing his fiddle.

At the end, Dad blew his nose. 'What a load of tosh,' he said, indistinctly.

'I thought it was lovely,' wept Mum, wiping her cheeks.

Everyone filed outside again, blinking in the evening sunshine. The wet scent of bluebells and lilac blossom mingled with the perfume of the yellow broom and the drooping flowers of the laburnum trees. Droplets of water glistened on the brown husks of spent daffodils.

Mum stood on an old plough. 'And now for the third thing,' she yelled.

'Quiet please,' shouted Dad. 'This will affect all of you.'

Gradually the chattering grew silent.

Mum said, 'The third thing is: Jo-Ellen's brother Mack is a film maker. He was so impressed with her research, and this glen, that he's asked if he can use our Museum as the location for the film he's making next spring. You'll have guessed it's to be called *Heartland* and you've just heard the story it's to be based on. The story of their ancestors, the MacKimbels of Auchentibart.'

Dad continued, 'And what's more, Mack's company has promised to restore the Auld Hoose for us, if we give permission. We're inclined to agree. A film would really put us on the tourist map. Visitors would flock here to see where it was made. It would tell the *world* that Glenmellish exists.'

Everyone cheered.

'There remains a mystery,' said Dad. 'Someone – we don't know who, but he must have been outstandingly strong – saved the lives of Annie and Duncan here. We'd like to thank him. If anyone knows to whom we owe this huge debt of gratitude, please tell us.'

Sadie leapt onto a trestle table littered with paper plates and puddings. Her face was covered in pink ice-cream. 'I can tell youse,' she yelled.

The crowd fell silent.

'Murdo Clerk,' she shouted. 'It wis Murdo.'

Annie caught sight of the big lad before everyone crowded round him. His face was scarlet with embarrassment. Soon, though, he was wreathed in smiles as first Mum and Dad, then everyone else went to congratulate him, clapping and shaking him by the hand.

Annie thanked him too. 'If it hadn't been for you, we'd have been burned alive,' she said, beginning to realise fully the horror of that night.

'It wisnae nothin'. I wis goin' hame, but this fella wouldnae let me gang up my road. He wis chuckin' stanes at me and that. I had tae turn back – and then I saw the fire.' Murdo looked perplexed.

For a moment Annie wondered if 'this fella' could have been Jock. Maybe, but it was Murdo's strength and quick action that had saved her life. What would she make of *her* time on earth? For one day it would come her turn to wither and die, like the daffodils. Or maybe she'd stay on here, a ghost playing around Auchentibart for ever, with Jock …

The ceilidh band struck up for a reel. Duncan joined in. Later they played Jock's tune and Annie felt happier than she could ever remember, until out of the corner of her eye she saw him looking wistfully in at the window.

How selfish she'd been. She'd kept putting off giving Jock his freedom because she liked having him around. But Duncan was right, she owed him. Now she must help him go free.

Next morning she got up at dawn. Blue, the puppy, stirred in his box as she dressed, then went back to sleep. Carefully she lifted the eggs out of the shirt and wrapped them in a warm towel. Folding the shirt into her jacket, she slipped silently out of the back door.

The air was cool and the sky streaked with pink clouds. Annie made her way past the empty hen run to the Auld

Hoose. Its blackened, empty windows filled her with gloom. She didn't want to say goodbye to Jock here.

Instead, she wandered up the course of the burn. Sure enough, it led her to the edge of the woods at Mairi's Well, where Jock had fixed up her wounded knee after the bike accident. Primroses and wild violets still grew among the dewy grass, laced with silvery cobwebs. The spring itself was a clear golden pool, the water riffling up gently from nowhere. No wonder folk used to think wells were magic places.

Annie remembered a picnic she'd had there with Duncan and Sadie.

'Where does the water come frae?' Sadie had asked.

'From underground. Maybe a hidden lake, there since the ice age.' Duncan had made his voice go spooky.

'Why sound so scary?' Annie had asked.

Duncan said, 'My gran says wells have got spirits.'

Now Annie lay gazing into the water. She could choose to make her eyes see through it to the pebbles, or change focus to the surface, where her own face looked back at her, a wobbly reflection. She hummed the old tune, thinking ...

Oh! Jock's face was there too in the pool, wavering about on the dazzle of sunlight.

She stood up. 'Jock?'

A flimsy shadow against the sun, he stepped from the pool of light and drifted towards her.

Annie scarcely breathed. She mustn't do anything to make him disappear.

He halted in front of her, his pale face streaked with dirt and tears.

She swallowed. Carefully, she pulled out his shirt and laid it on the ground between them.

Quietly she began to tell him everything she knew. She

told of finding the sickle in the tree, of how she would like to keep it forever. She told him she'd *seen* how Black Alastair had accidentally hit his head on the tree, so Jock was innocent of any crime. She told him about the minister who had buried him and prayed for his soul. And she told him how much she herself would miss him.

Purple clouds were filling up the sky beyond the Museum. Far away, down Loch Mellish, lilac-coloured drifts of rain swept towards the land. Little shivers of wind whispered among the trees behind her, though the sun still shone.

A rainbow began to grow from a curving stalk of colour, growing stronger all the time. It was the best rainbow she'd ever seen, a crescent of purple, blue, yellow, green, pink, scarlet and orange standing above the little pool, almost near enough for her to touch. In the centre of all that brilliant colour, Jock's thin shadow held out his arms.

Gradually others appeared, a growing crowd of wispy figures all dancing round the well. One could have been his mother, folding him in her arms then birling him round. Snatches of song and wild music came towards Annie, then faded till only Jock remained.

He spoke so softly she could have been imagining the sound. '*Feumaidh tu cluas a thoirt dhan ghaoith dhomh a-nist, feuch an lorg thu mi eadar na frasan agus gathan na grèine, thoir sùil gheur air na boillsgeaidhean beaga a dh'fhalbhas air feadh nan duilleagean.* Listen for me now in the wind, see me in the showers o' rain, in the sunbeams, in the stars, in the wee glints o' licht amang the leaves.' Slowly he bent, picked up his shirt and slid it over his head. It flapped around his frame, becoming transparent as dragonfly wings. His voice was fading away and the rainbow was paling to pastels. 'I'll awa' then, b*eannachd leat*, Annie, b*eannachd leat an dràsda, beannachdan* … fareweel,' and his words were softer than the breeze, as the sunlight died and the rainbow vanished.

A pure white deer stood there, gazing at her.

The sudden cloudburst took Annie by surprise, icy raindrops splashing on her head, pouring down her neck, running in rivulets down her back and into her shoes. 'Jock,' she called. 'Jock, don't go, don't leave me!'

The deer turned and fled into the forest.

Now there was only the rain.

* * *

Today, after Annie finishes drying her hair, she calls, 'Time to go out, puppy.'

Workmen are coming to make the Auld Hoose safe. But before they come, she'll take one last look at the burned-out ruins.

She wanders through the ashes thinking; it's so great we're staying on here after all. Oh, there's the sickle, sticking out of the ground. It's beside the lintel stone which must have fallen from the doorway when the roof caved in.

Annie sits on the long flat stone, fingering its rough markings. She realises writing is carved into the surface! The charring makes it difficult to see. Guessing some of the letters, she reads, *Here lies Jock, being the last Nic-Caimbeil of Glenmellish, departed this life 17 September 1851 aged fourteen years.* Jock's gravestone, 'borrowed' from the graveyard by someone for the rebuilding of the Auld Hoose!

She thinks; I'm glad Jock chose me to help find out about his mum and everything – and I'm glad we did and that he's free. And I'm *sure* that was him in Jo-Ellen's film, making faces at Sadie, laughing and dancing to Duncan's music on Gala Day. Anyway, my friend Jock, you *can't* leave me. Why?

'Cos you're stuck in my memory forever. And so, everything's all right.'

END

If you enjoyed *The Ghost of Glenmellish*, you might like *Stranger on the River*, also by PAT GERBER.

It's an adventure story about salmon poaching. Sadie Munro's pal Valentine overhears Bloodshot plotting to poison the river and steal the salmon. Is Coll involved? How can Valentine save the river without damaging their friendship for ever?

Stranger on the River got great reviews from children, like it's 'a real nail-biter', 'good for both boys and girls', 'a book you just won't put down'. Teachers said: 'There were so many aspects we could relate to the curriculum – environmental issues, the Scottish flavour, the comparison between town and country life.'